MURDER,

Relatively Speaking

Helen C. Ayers

Other Books by this Author

Appalachian Daughter, April, 2006

The Stuff of Legends, November, 2006

MURDER, Relatively Speaking, March 2010

Grandma's Brown County Cookbook, October, 2015

Devil's Halo, February, 2021

Granny Goes to the Cruise Ship (Granny Goosefoot Adventures Book 1), May, 2021

Granny Goosefoot Goes to New York (Granny Goosefoot Adventures), December, 2022

Harriet Goes to Dinner, August, 2022

The Frog and the Toad, February, 2023

The Bird Who Could Not Sing, July 2023

This Is Our Brown County Then 1800-1900: Revering Our Past, August, 2023

Being Healthy Can Kill You: Reading This Book Could Save Your Life, September 2023

The books are available online
or any bookseller can order them for you.

You may order direct by writing to: Books

7256 Keith Donaldson Road.

Freetown, IN 47235

MURDER,

*Relatively
Speaking*

Helen C. Ayers

Dedication

This book is dedicated to the memory of all those who have lost their lives due to domestic violence. This crime is a scourge on our society today. But there is help for those who feel their lives are being threatened. The help is as near as the local sheriff's department, prosecutor's office, judge, religious leader, schoolteacher, friends, and your own medical doctor.

All these advocates of domestic tolerance take domestic violence very seriously and act accordingly and speedily so call one of them immediately if you feel threatened.

The most important thing you can do to protect yourself from domestic violence is to remove yourself from the area of conflict. Any of the above sources and many others stand ready to assist you.

There are safe houses you can go to and take your children for a limited stay at no cost to you while you are directed around the system and reorganize your life.

Many of the victims discussed in this book may have been saved if they had only known about these safe houses, but these events related to you in the book happened long before the advent of safe houses.

Thanks

I would like to thank all my friends who keep telling me to write stories. With encouragement from them I find the words to say what they want me to say.

I would also like to especially thank my husband, my sons and especially my grandchildren who are my greatest source of strength and love.

Table of Contents

Chapter 1

It was one of those miserably cold, windy and wet November days he dreaded worse every year. All Charlie wanted to do was prop his feet on the fender of the wood stove with a cup of coffee in one hand and a good book in the other to while away the afternoon hours. One of those nice fish sandwiches in the kitchen would go very well too, he thought, savoring the anticipation of that treat he was reserving for later.

It had been drizzling rain for several days and the drenching rain and cold, almost gale-force wind had knocked off every last leaf from the big hardwood trees in the yard. The sky now had that cold lowering grayish cast to it that foretold more cold miserable winter weather was just around the corner.

The wind blowing through the eaves and down the chimney of the big log house shook the old place almost to its foundation, making eerie haunting sounds as it rumbled through holes into the attic spaces.

"I really need to do some fixing up around here," Charlie thought to himself as he prepared to leave the warm confines of his living room for the gloomy outdoors to rake up into piles those infernal dead leaves. "It sounds like a freight train moving through the attic. What will it be like later on in the winter," he wondered. God, he hated Midwest winters with a passion.

"I'm spending next winter somewhere warm where there aren't any leaves to rake, snakes to kill and wives to make happy," he swore to himself. Where was his wife anyway? She had been here earlier and dropped off the fish sandwiches but was now gone again having left those sandwiches on the kitchen counter for him to eat for his supper whenever he got hungry. It was getting harder and harder for him to even afford that treat, but his wife didn't know that yet.

God she is stupid, he thought, thinking of his wife, Gerry. "I wish Mabel was here with me right now. Now there is one sweet woman," he dreamed. But his wife surely would not like that idea, he considered, remembering how she had reacted one other time when she had caught him and Mabel in the very act. Lord, she was mad, he remembered as he stood shaking his head.

The tall, lanky, dark-haired and handsome man decided he deserved both a climate and a wife better than he had. He just could not afford either one right now and that made him mad. Where has all my hard-earned money gone, he wondered to himself for about the thousandth time as he pushed himself up out of his easy chair to prepare to go outside.

But the demands of the neighborhood required that he shrug himself into his old fleece-lined denim mackinaw, don a pair of leather work gloves, a warm thick cap and go out and rake the last of the dead leaves and fallen twigs from the lawn. It was a loathsome chore he hated. Why one of those sorry boys of ours couldn't do this job just once and not leave all the work to me was a question he could not answer, he thought to himself.

But raking and burning the leaves had an upside too. The smell of burning leaves was a pleasant one that still wafted in his memories from childhood. He loved the smell of burning leaves so he guessed he would do the chore.

He recalled how as a child he had raked the leaves into monstrous piles then grabbed up a hound dog in his arms and took long jumps and landed right into the middle of the piles. Once he had played all he wanted to with his dogs in the leaves, he would then re-rake them back into piles and burn them. This was the smell he could recall at will.

The impossibly large yard with its grove of maple, ash, walnut, poplar and sycamore trees contributed literally tons of dry brittle leaves and twigs every year and Charlie worked diligently making huge piles to burn later that evening when the wind had died down. The rain they had been having had also knocked down a fair number of small limbs. All would go into his burn pile, he thought. "Too bad I don't have some hot dogs ready to roast over the fire," he thought. Charlie had been raking for about an hour and a half when his favorite cousin, Jim, upon seeing Charlie working outside, stopped by on his way home from work to chat with him for a few minutes. They chatted awhile as Charlie leaned on his rake resting, then,

3

getting his second wind he invited Jim to come inside and share a fish sandwich and some hot coffee with him.

"Come on in, you can stay a few more minutes," Charlie urged his cousin, but Jim demurred.

"No, I really can't come in today, I have to get on home or the little woman will kill me if I am late for supper again. Today is our fortieth wedding anniversary and she has prepared a big feast probably," he explained and unlike Charlie, he was actually looking forward to seeing his wife of forty years.

Unknown to him it was the most fortuitous decision Jim would make in his lifetime. Two hours later he would receive word that his cousin Charlie was dead, killed by his own hand and his body burned in his garage. Charlie was found after the fire was extinguished, his body burned nearly to a crisp with his best shotgun lying across what little was left of his chest. Short stumps of his extremities survived the fire but none of his soft pelvic and abdominal organs did. In fact, there was so little body remaining it was difficult to say for sure that this actually was a human body.

Jim had always envied Charlie. It seemed to him like everything Charlie touched turned to gold and they had started off pretty evenly in life. "Don't hardly seem fair," Jim thought as he hurriedly drove his old truck to his cousin's house to see if he could help.

But Jim hadn't had the visions of wealth and prestige his cousin Charlie had. Whatever Charlie wanted he attempted to get and usually succeeded. Jim was much slower in both thought and action and never hurried unless he was gently prodded by someone else.

Charlie and his brother Chad together had once owned a big general store that carried everything from lumber to hardware to soft goods and items for the nearby farms including various poisons, the sale of which was not yet regulated by the government. It was the largest store of its kind in the area, and the brothers had made a small fortune in that business before Charlie started making noises about wanting to sell it. "I want to try something else now," he had told Chad.

Finally deciding to go on to greener pastures he sold his share of the general store to his equally popular brother who would run the store alone for several years after the sale while Charlie pursued his other interests.

Charlie took the money from the sale of his half of the store and built condominiums and apartment buildings, the first of their kind in Green County. Since they were the first of their kind in the area, they were very popular, and they brought him still another fortune before he sold that enterprise to his insurance company that had provided the financing for this project and to whom he owed a large sum of money.

It seemed to his friends that Charlie just could not lose at anything he turned his hand to but only he, his lawyer and the insurance company knew about the enormous debt he owed. Rising flood waters last spring had swamped a third of his apartments forcing him to spend vast sums of money he did not actually have, and he had had to borrow from the insurance company to repair the damages done by the flood waters to the lower-level apartments. The two upper floors were not damaged by the flood waters but had to be vacated until the lower floor had been refurbished and he received an occupancy permit from the plan commission to reopen. Not only were the repairs very expensive, but there was also the lost income from all the apartments of the entire complex. This income represented tens of thousands of dollars to Charlie.

But despite his problems Charlie had continued to spend money like there would not be a worry tomorrow, buying large luxury cars for himself, his sons and his wife. His wife Geraldine, or Gerry as he referred to her, wore only the finest clothes on her back and had a mink coat to wear when they went out in public. But all his buying power was gained through mortgaging everything his friends figured he owned outright. Only he, his attorney and his insurance company knew the entire extent of his debt.

Charlie loved to see Gerry dressed up because with her clothes and his money and with her hair done up at the beauty shop, she could still look really smart. He secretly hated her, but she would never know that. He liked it when he saw envy on the faces of the wives of the other men in their crowd when she wore these fine clothes. Charlie believed if you were rich, you should definitely show it.

But secretly, in his dreams, he always saw Mabel Miller wearing that fur coat, never Gerry. "Oh, how I love to make love to that woman," he mused thinking of Mabel.

Gerry enjoyed her luxuries, but she was not addicted to them as Charlie was. Yes, she enjoyed their large spacious custom-designed log home, the covered bridge he had built over the small creek which ran through their property as an entrance to their estate and her big comfortable Lincoln Town Car with its heated seats. But as little as she drove anymore, the beautiful white car got few miles put on the odometer. Someone was usually present to drive her wherever she wanted to go.

Sometimes though, she wished they weren't rich. She actually had enjoyed her life much better when it was just her and Charlie and the boys having a good time together. "Now I never get to see very much of him, or the boys either for that matter, now that they are grown," she realized.

Their main house contained only three bedrooms and a couple of baths. There was another house built about 400 yards from the main house that

Helen C. Ayers

contained another eight bedrooms. Each of those bedrooms also had its own private in-suite bath, sitting room and railed balcony for their many visitors to enjoy.

The main house also contained a ballroom where the governor and other big shots they knew around the state would be invited to dance the night away while a nice dance band played; and a library filled with hundreds of leather-bound best sellers on tall shelves reaching to the ceiling which had never been opened and read. A detached 4-car garage was there also for their personal cars. It was this garage that would become Charlie's funeral pyre.

How he could have started the fire after he shot himself was the $64,000 question all the police and his friends wanted the answer to.

Charlie was losing money rapidly now and had been for quite some time even though most of his friends had no inkling he was so far in debt, and he had hated that. He could not bear to appear a failure before his friends because he had always been on top when the contests were over.

Now there had been that horrific fire inside his garage and a body had been found burned beyond recognition. Was that body Charlie's?

Had he committed suicide? Was he depressed? His friends would report to the police that he had been somewhat depressed lately, but nothing really bad.

"We all get depressed sometimes," one of his friends was heard to say as the firemen attempted to douse the last hot spots of the fire.

Maybe he had gone to the garage to get fire starter of some sort for the leaf burning project and accidentally caught the garage on fire, the firemen mused. But if it was an accident, how come there was a shotgun lying across his chest? A preliminary examination of the body by the funeral director did not show any gunshot wound. All this was very puzzling to the bystanders.

These were just many of the questions remaining as the firemen doused the last of the flames and began sorting through the ashes.

Now this fire department was typical of most rural fire departments everywhere in rural counties all over America. They operated short-handed and without all the necessary equipment most large departments take for granted. Some of the firemen were not terribly bright either and many lacked sophisticated training, but they recognized a burned body when they found one in the ashes so perhaps they weren't too stupid at that.

Prior to this fire, one of the firemen had been quoted extensively in the local newspaper as saying, "We haven't lost a foundation yet." That statement would follow him to his grave as would the mistakes made this night by the firemen and the police investigators.

No effort was made to secure the scene once the fire was doused and the body found and removed. Neighbors and bystanders walked freely through the debris, kicking some of it out of their way and picking up and carrying away other bits of souvenir evidence as they went.

The remains of the victim had been found and solemnly placed inside a body bag by the son of the local funeral home director who would take the remains there to be buried hurriedly in a few days. That was all that was left of poor Charlie when he was found.

No one, not a single soul, doubted that burned body was all that was left of poor Charlie. There was no medical examiner in the county to check the body. Only the funeral home management, who also served as the local elected coroner, would be in charge. No formal forensic training was required to be a coroner. All it took was a willingness to serve and a name easily recognizable on the ballot. This father and son team switched jobs after every second election since no one else wanted it and they could only serve two consecutive four-year terms without a break according to law. And since theirs was the only funeral home in the entire rural county, these two men were "it." No autopsy was planned because everyone "knew" it was Charlie in that fire.

Only the son of the funeral home owner had his doubts. Those doubts would be the catalyst for a long drawn out many-years-long mystery. Right then however, if someone said, "This is Charlie," then Charlie it was. His few charred remains were summarily buried a couple of days later with all the pomp due a distinguished citizen of the tiny community of Stoneville. A small tombstone was later erected with the proper information inscribed naming the grave that of Charlie and listing his birth and death dates. Nothing more elaborate was done to mark this site as the final resting place of one of Stoneville's most envied and distinguished citizens.

He was a thirty-third degree Mason, belonged to the country club, the proper local Protestant church and was well-known and respected in the community, so his send-off was a fine one. It was just his marker that was a bit plain and scant.

His cousin Jim was heard to say, "Charlie would really have liked his send- off. He was a great one for a good show."

But good old cousin Charlie was not destined to rest long in his solitary grave.

Jake, the undertaker's son, still fretted and talked the matter over almost daily with his dad, George, as they sat around and awaited the next burial to be brought to their attention. "Dad, I just don't know if that was Charlie or not. Too many things just don't add up," Jake told his dad many times.

11

Now George, who was the current coroner, was of the old school which said "leave well enough alone."

The two dickered back and forth for about two months before George finally gave in and agreed with Jake to dig the body up and have an autopsy done at a nearby teaching hospital.

"I just didn't like things being undecided like that. It made me very nervous," Jake often said much later.

"There was a gun across his chest, but I never found a gunshot wound, and it just didn't seem to be the right size to be Charlie." Jake had known Charlie his entire lifetime, both having grown up in this tiny community of mostly small farmers, and they were of nearly the same age.

Gerry, by then, had already notified the insurance company that poor Charlie was dead, enclosing a brief little note that asked them to please send her the two million dollars that was due to be paid to her.

"No way," the insurance company agent responded. "We have no proof, other than your word, that it was Charlie."

Gerry finally filed a lawsuit against the insurance company asking that the money due her be paid to her. Her husband was dead, and she wanted her two million dollars plus interest. It seemed like a done deal to her, but a trial date would be set for way in the future.

Gerry was furious when she learned the funeral home director and his son had sought and obtained a court order for exhumation of Charlie's poor bones. "That is Charlie in there, you have no right to dig him back up," she screamed at them as they kept digging.

But according to the coroner they did have the right to do that. Once it is believed a crime has been committed, the body no longer belongs to the family they explained to Gerry. The coroner and medical examiner have first dibs on the body.

Finally, Gerry's son Fred led her from the grave site and put her in his Ferrari. "Come on Mom, damn it, settle down, let them dig, they can't prove anything," he assured her.

Gerry had been at this son's house to visit a bit after bringing some fish sandwiches back from a popular fish stand in a nearby county. It was there the police had found her and told her about the fire in their garage and that they believed her husband had died in the flames.

"Oh, no," she had cried. "Not my poor Charlie. I can't believe this."

Fred had placed his mom in her Lincoln, and they had sped to her home which was up a narrow lane about five miles from his own home.

Arriving at the fire scene, she had jumped from the car, screaming for Charlie and with tears flowing from her eyes, fell onto her knees on the freshly raked lawn and wept for the husband who was no more.

It was a good show, and a believable one. Everyone knew how good Charlie had been to Gerry. "Why, just look at that big splashy car he bought her and all those fine clothes," they said.

The neighbors were basically kind people and they felt sorry for Gerry. She was apparently absolutely devastated by Charlie's death.

It was a long time after what was left of Charlie's body had been removed and the firemen had gone before Gerry informed her sons she would be remaining in her house that night.

"Mom, you can't do that, come and go back home with me," Fred implored her, but she refused to listen.

The fire had not damaged her log house, only the detached garage, she informed him. There was no reason she could see for staying away from home. She was a remarkably strong-willed woman so Fred let her stay there alone.

He had been worried the stress of the fire and the death of his father would cause her to have a diabetic reaction and she might need his help. She assured him she would call if she needed him during the night.

Gerry laid her plans after everyone had gone, leaving her alone to mourn her late husband in the privacy of their home.

Little did any of her neighbors, friends or family know how much she privately hated Charlie. They did not know that she had come home one afternoon and found him in bed with another woman whose name she had pried from Charlie's lips. It was none other than the Mabel Miller he had been mooning over while he was raking leaves.

Gerry had made a solemn oath to Charlie that afternoon that she would get even with him for betraying her with that floozy if it was the last thing she ever did and tonight she would fulfill that promise.

It was not a restful night for Gerry at all. She worked like a crazy woman nearly all night long putting her plans into action until along toward morning she finally called Fred back and said she was having trouble with her diabetes and could he come and take her to the hospital.

Dutiful son Fred sped to her side, whisked her into her car, and drove her to a nearby hospital. Dr. Freedman, the doctor on call, did not find very much amiss with her and after giving her some orange juice to drink, sent her home.

When they returned in the early morning hours after daybreak, they found her property swarming with cops again. Gerry and Fred were both unaware the funeral director's son had asked the cops to investigate further.

The local sheriff, who was another of Charlie's brothers, along with state police agents were raking around in the ashes but would not tell Gerry and Fred what they were looking for. Evidence was haphazardly sorted and bagged then later, the remainder of the garage debris was hauled to the nearby county dump and disposed of.

In the ashes a few feet from where they had found the remains of Charlie the previous night, they found a gold Masonic ring. It was found buried way down deep in the ashes underneath a scorched board, hardly damaged at all. The gold band with the large diamond was nearly as good as new and would appear to the unsuspecting bystander to be the one he normally wore.

No wallet or other identifying information other than the ring was found. After half-heartedly looking around and kicking through the fire debris, the investigators left.

Gerry breathed a sigh of relief. She was so glad they were gone; maybe she could get back to normal now.

Jake, the undertaker's son, knew Charlie so well he knew what kind of ring he normally wore. Charlie was proud of that ring and it was very distinctive. Something about the one they had found just did not ring true with him.

"I don't believe that is the ring Charlie was always flashing," he told his dad. "And why wasn't it melted? Most of that body was burned away. Gold melts really easy yet the ring was hardly damaged. I know there is something wrong here," he fretted.

Several things about the condition of the body and other pieces of evidence worried Jake around the clock. He could not sleep. All he could do was worry and fret that something was being overlooked.

What clue am I overlooking, he wondered. That body did belong to Charlie, didn't it? Everybody but me couldn't be wrong, could they? And Charlie had not been seen since the fire so it must have been him, he concluded. But the case still bothered Jake.

Jake was not the coroner, his father was and his father absolutely refused to change his mind. He had signed a death certificate saying Charlie was dead and by Ned he was going to stay dead.

Jake had been elected coroner at the election earlier that month but had not as yet taken office. He would do that beginning January 1. Until that time, he would just be patient. He hated to go against his dad, but he just felt he was right. He did not believe the remains they had buried was Charlie. But if it wasn't Charlie, then who was it?

A couple of days after he took over the office of coroner, he told his dad he was going to exhume the body and have an autopsy done on it.

His father tried to talk him out of the idea, but now Jake had the power to do what he had been dying to do ever since the fire.

17

The two of them approached the local judge and explained Jake's doubts. Judge Stearn finally agreed the body should be exhumed and an autopsy performed on it. An order of exhumation and autopsy was signed by Judge Stearn.

That was what happened and when Gerry and Fred heard about the order they had sped to the cemetery. A snitch at the courthouse had gotten word to them of what was going down.

Both were adamantly against the idea, but the judge had the upper hand. The body no longer belonged to Gerry and Fred anymore, it belonged to the police, he told them believing a crime had been committed. An autopsy would be done and there was nothing they could do to stop it.

Speculation just got deeper and deeper as to what had actually happened, how it had happened and who it had happened to.

The local weekly newspaper had a field day, putting out a special edition— the first in its 100 year history—with screaming headlines announcing that the body was being exhumed.

The editor, a wimpy mama's boy with round coke-bottle glasses on his face, was new on the job and he was building a subscriber base. This story should help him a lot.

It wasn't that he disliked Charlie at all. Charlie had stopped in the office on numerous occasions to shoot the breeze with him. George just felt he had to take advantage of all the breaking news items and build that subscriber base to impress his dad, himself a long-time newspaper man he was trying to emulate. His father had bought the newspaper for him as a gift and George really wanted to do a good job.

Headlines would blaze for weeks. The fire and the man's body found in the fire was a topic of never ending interest at every local bar and diner as the locals speculated about who it was and where good old Charlie was hiding out if he had not died in the fire.

By now the word was out that Charlie had murdered someone and placed his body in the fire to make it look like he had committed suicide. There was no suicide clause in his insurance policy and two million dollars looked pretty good to him, they said.

Everybody in the county now knew he had been in deep poo-poo financially. "Those boys of his are bleeding him dry," they assured each other. Other financial investments he had made had uncharacteristically failed and now were being made public. Had he really lost his Midas touch, the wags wondered?

"Why, they let them take all the evidence and throw it in the dump," they chortled to each other.

"Gerry's gonna be one rich widder," another said. "I might need to get on her good side, marry her myself. I could use some of that money."

The state police trooper investigating the alleged crime made so many bloopers and mistakes in his investigation that by now everyone was convinced the truth would never be known. This first trooper would later be replaced by a much more efficient trooper who would spend the rest of his law enforcement career trying to untangle the web which was spun out of this fire. Not many of the locals had much use for the state police, but the state police had to be called in because the sheriff at the time was a brother of Charlie's. "You all know he would be on his brother's side," was the rumor flying about tiny Stoneville.

Everyone, it seemed, was on Charlie's side. If he did it, they seemed to want him to get away with it. It didn't make a lot of difference to them who was in the fire if it wasn't Charlie. Nobody else was reported missing so it must not be too important who it was who had burned to a cinder. They all liked good time Charlie. Hadn't he bought every one of them a beer at one time or another at the local watering hole, or loaned them some money when they were down and out?"

Another man said he didn't like insurance companies anyway. "I had a claim one time and they never paid me a dang penny. Insurance companies are just as bad as most lawyers. I hope she gets everything she deserves from them," the old timer was heard to say.

For months, whenever two or more gathered for coffee or beer in Stoneville, the subject of what had happened to Charlie came up. Everyone, it seemed, had their own theory.

Finally the autopsy report came back. The foremost forensic expert in the state said the man in the fire had died of smoke inhalation, not a shotgun wound. The man had only one kidney and his blood type was AB positive and the man was about six inches shorter than old Charlie had been. It could not have been Charlie.

I know Charlie had type B blood, not AB, a family member said. "I remember seeing it on his military ID a long time ago and on his dog tags too." "As far as I know he had two kidneys," another relative said. "I never heard any differently from anyone in the family. Course he has never been sick so there is no need to check his kidneys before now."

The noted forensic pathologist had signed a new death certificate certifying the deceased was "John Doe." Charlie's wife and sons were furious. The body's remains were duly cremated and reburied in the same grave at the local cemetery and no changes were made on the tombstone.

"That is our Dad and we will prove it," son Fred swore.

That was when Gerry had written to the insurance company and demanded they send her the money they owed her. If not, she would sue. Now knowing that the pathologist had signed a new death certificate saying that the body was not Charlie but a John Doe, they told her to sue away and she had done so.

Gerry eventually became a pathetic figure around town. Going from riches to rags was hard on her. It was not nearly as much fun as going from rags to riches had been.

Instead of the mink coat, she was reduced to wearing a thin and shabby cotton coat. In place of the fine silk and wool dresses and suits she favored, she now wore polyester hand-me-downs that she bought at the local Goodwill Store. Her Lincoln had been repossessed by the bank long ago and she was now driving a rusted out small Ford car given to her by a relative.

And the fine log home she had been accustomed to living in was no longer hers either. The bank Charlie had owed so much money to had already taken possession of it and a banker's family now lived in her old home. Her generous nephew, Shorty Long, allowed her to live in a rundown house he owned that was little more than a tar paper shack. It was really decrepit, but it had a roof over it, so Gerry took it.

It would be a long, cold unfruitful day she would wait to collect her money— money she tried to convince everyone she knew that she deserved.

Chapter 2

Months passed after the first fire and it seemed every day brought to light a new problem for Gerry. She was so tired of fighting the system; all she wanted was her insurance money. No one knew how hard she had worked to earn that money.

It had now been several months since she had filed the lawsuit to get her money the insurance company owed her for Charlie being dead, but the company refused to pay her a dime. "Show us proof," they always challenged.

In the meantime, the local prosecuting attorney (PA) had taken the case of the dead man before Judge Stearn and asked that an arrest warrant be issued charging Charlie with murder. The motion was granted, and Charlie became a fugitive from justice which infuriated Gerry further.

"How can they charge a dead man with murder," she angrily asked anyone who would listen.

But the warrant for murder, believed committed by Charlie, would not be recalled. If he was ever found, he would have to stand trial for murder because there was no statute of limitations on the crime of murder.

Gerry thought that by bombarding the local newspaper with letters to the editor demanding that a coroner's inquest be held to identify the body they found in the fire and buried in the local cemetery as her husband Charlie would force the issue so that she could get satisfaction. But the local officials remained unswayed, and the judge was beginning to get very annoyed with Gerry.

After receiving letters like this every few weeks for months and years on end, the local newspaper finally refused to print them. The letters didn't build the subscriber base anymore as they once had, made George no money, and just used up valuable space his staff could sell to advertisers. Other stories were now filling the pages of the local weekly newspaper. Unless there was a break in the case, Gerry and her dead husband were no longer news.

"You have no proof that body was Charlie," she was told by George. "We can't keep printing the same letter over and over, nor can we try the case in the paper."

An attorney in a nearby city volunteered to assist Gerry in her cause without charging her a fee. If successful, attorney Samuel Rogerson would receive one-third of any money she was awarded. Filled with avarice, Mr. Rogerson was thinking that one-third of two million dollars would be just under $700,000 plus any interest awarded by the judge. Not a bad haul by any means.

Mr. Rogerson advised Gerry to search her house for any proof of her husband's blood type. She searched frantically for weeks. Finally, Eureka! Gerry found Charlie's wallet. It had fallen down behind the couch cushions, she told her attorney. His military ID was still intact inside one of the little picture windows and it showed he had the same blood type as the deceased. Neither her attorney nor any of the county officials knew that the couch in her home was not the same one she had owned when she lived with Charlie. That too, had been repossessed after the first fire.

There was no proof her husband had only one kidney, but the blood type appeared to match, she told him.

The wallet was taken to court and shown to the judge who looked at it warily.

"How long have you had this," Judge Stearn asked Gerry.

"I just found it the other day, down behind the couch cushion," she replied. "Well, we will have to keep this for evidence," Judge Stearn said.

"But can you tell me now that that body was my Charlie so I can get my money," she asked?

"No, I'm sorry, I cannot do that, but I would like to talk to your attorney in my chambers," Judge Stearn told Gerry.

Mr. Rogerson followed the judge to his chambers behind the courtroom and closed the door.

He sat stiffly on the leading edge of an old oak chair as Judge Stearn seated himself behind the desk.

"What's up?" Rogerson asked the judge.

"What's up is, the gig is up," Judge Stearn told him. "That military ID has been altered. I am sure if we sent it to a laboratory that it would show that." "I know Mrs. Jones wants us to believe the deceased was her husband, but this ID sure doesn't prove that," he told Mr. Rogerson.

"And why did she wait all this time to suddenly present this," he asked. "She told me she had just found it," Rogerson replied. "I rushed right over here with her to file it with the court."

"Is your client willing to have her sons' own blood drawn to compare with the deceased," Judge Stearn questioned.

"That would prove whether it was possible for this man to be her husband and the father of her children, based upon these blood types."

"I don't know, but I will find out and get back to you," Mr. Rogerson said. "Do that and quit taking up my valuable court time with these frivolous matters," Judge Stearn rebuked him. "I will not put up with any more of your shenanigans."

Mr. Rogerson returned to the courtroom to find Gerry patiently waiting. She was dressed today in a rather fusty faintly pink polyester dress which zipped up the front. She was carrying a navy-blue plastic purse which she held on to with both hands as it sat in her lap. Her hair was uncombed and messy, and she was beginning to have some pretty bad looking sores on her face. Were those sores scratches, Rogerson wondered. Did she scratch her face as a result of her nerves? Her shoes were of the cheapest variety, and everything taken altogether just leant an air of destitution to her appearance.

"God, I wish I had known her when she was supposed to have been pretty and rich," he thought to himself.

When the state police and local sheriff had searched her home for evidence, they had removed every picture of the couple from her photo albums and kept those pictures as possible evidence. Rogerson did not have a single picture of Gerry in her heyday.

He had never yet had the opportunity to see what she looked like dressed up in nice clothes and with her hair styled.

"How quickly one can go downhill," he thought, but he was all smiles when he greeted her again.

"What did he want," she demanded.

"Well," Rogerson hedged, "He wanted to keep the wallet with the ID until your insurance trial date is set. They will need it then. And, he wanted me to ask you if the boys would be willing to have their blood drawn for a blood type match."

'No way. I would not ask them to let anyone stick needles in them," she said. "That wallet has his blood type, that's all they need."

"You need to tell him to mind his own business and say that was my Charlie," she demanded. "Then I can get my money," she said as she stomped out of the courtroom.

Wishing to himself that things could be that easy and that simple, attorney Rogerson followed.

Chapter 3

That evening Gerry called her sons to come to her home for a meeting and when they arrived she explained what the judge said he wanted her to do. "Now Mom, you know we don't want anyone poking around in this," Fred said.

"Well," she asked, "How are we going to prove it was Charlie, then?" "If I don't get any money, you don't get any money," she challenged them. Three madder men could not have been found.

It was mere weeks after their father had died when each of their fancy automobiles had been repossessed by the finance companies and banks where they had been used as collateral by their father to get money for his latest get-rich-quick schemes.

Her youngest son, Adam, was now sitting in the county jail awaiting trial on voluntary manslaughter charges so was unavailable to be at this meeting. It had been an accident, he claimed, that he had accidentally shot and killed a deer hunter behind his mom's house but even though he said it was an accident, the new sheriff believed he meant to kill this young man.

"If that stupid brother of ours hadn't messed up so badly, we might all be rich men right now," John, the second son said.

"Now, don't go blaming your brother for that accident," his mother admonished him. "He was just trying to do what you boys told him to do."

"I told him to get rid of that hunter and not let another on this place. What does he do but shoot him dead. That was not my plan, and it only drew the police to our property again. He is just stupid. I nearly wet my pants when I saw the hunter's body," Barney said.

"Well, you all knew we could have these kinds of problems. Don't be too hard on Adam now," she pleaded.

Fred had arrived one morning a month or so ago to see his mother and to ask if she had any money she could lend him. When he arrived he found his younger brother sitting at the kitchen table drinking the first of many cups of coffee he would drink that day.

Adam told Fred he had heard a gunshot back in the woods about the time he had gotten out of bed.

"And you haven't been back there to check it out?" Fred demanded. "No, I just figured it was a deer hunter. It is the first day of the season," Adam explained.

"You stupid little cur. Get your rifle and get back in those woods and take care of the matter right now; run him off," Fred had exploded as he slung the now empty coffee mug against the kitchen wall splintering the cup in a thousand pieces.

Adam who had always been afraid of his older, stronger brother, had quickly donned his parka, boots and knit cap for the walk back into the woods behind his mom's new digs.

Creeping up on the hunters, he stood behind a tree until he could see clearly. He slowly raised the rifle to firing position and aimed it at the hunter. When the rifle fired, the hunter dropped like a stone, screaming to someone that he had been shot. It was only then that Adam realized there were two men in those woods; a father and son team he would later learn.

The father saw Adam running away and called to him to stop.

Adam yelled back that he was going to call the ambulance and would be back as soon as he could, that he hadn't meant to hit the guy. 'It was an accident," he yelled back, "I thought he was a deer."

Once outside the visual range of the hunters, Adam slowed down considerably. He had not known there were two men in the woods. He had seen only the one and he had meant to leave no witnesses.

Adam wasn't sure the wounded man would die, but he had aimed for the heart. Not taking into account the descent of the hill on the victim before him, he had actually shot the young man through his left thigh, severing his femoral artery. By the time Adam reached his mother's house, it was too late to call for the ambulance. The young man he had shot was already dead from blood loss and his father was grief stricken.

There were no ambulances as such in the small county. The county, like many other rural areas across the country at that time, still relied solely on the hearse from the local funeral home to transport the ill and injured to the hospital as well as the dead to the area's only funeral home.

It made the funeral home more money to transport the dead directly to their own facility, so they had been known to slow down their response time in hopes of improving their own financial picture.

That was the case that day. They delayed long enough in responding to the emergency call from the Jones house to fill their hearse's tank with gas before leaving Stoneville. It was just long enough to allow the young man to die in the woods, but nothing could be proven.

The fact they were being called to the Jones home again was just ironic to them.

After arriving at the house, they asked Adam and his brothers to accompany them into the wooded area where the victim lay to show where he was and to help carry the heavy gurney. They had just returned from the woods, but they agreed to assist the funeral director in carrying the heavy gurney to the site where the young man was lying.

Upon arrival they discovered him lying dead in a large pool of blood with his grief-stricken father on his knees crying and rocking back and forth onto his heels beside him. The young man's heart had stopped beating only after it had successfully pumped the man's blood from his body. The dark, already congealing pool of blood was large and the body very pale.

"You killed my son," the father screamed at Adam. "I saw you." "No," Adam yelled back, "I swear I didn't kill him."

Jake, the funeral director, told John and Fred to go back to the house and call the sheriff. "I want him here right now," they were told.

The brothers took off once again at a trot back to the house. It would be hours later before the sheriff completed his investigation. The sheriff in office now was not the boys' uncle. That uncle had been defeated in the November election. This was a newer, tougher sheriff. The family knew him, of course, since they knew nearly everyone in the small county, but he was not related; a rare fact indeed for these parts. Nearly everyone was related somehow it seemed.

As the sheriff prepared to leave, he placed handcuffs on Adam after pulling his hands behind his back and placed him in the back seat of his patrol car.

"Why are you taking Adam to jail," Gerry yelled at the Sheriff. "He told you this was an accident and he had not intentionally killed anybody."

"You better call him a lawyer," the Sheriff advised Gerry. "He's gonna need one. That man's father said he saw Adam shoot his son and I believe him. I'm charging Adam with voluntary manslaughter."

On that response, the Sheriff parked his stout body behind the wheel of his patrol car and drove away, leaving Gerry crying in the yard.

"What more can happen to us," Gerry wondered.

That's exactly what the other boys wondered as they gathered round their mother's kitchen table that morning.

It seemed like every day now it was another new problem for her to work on. Now her favorite son, "baby" Adam, 24-years-old, was in jail. It would fall upon her shoulders to see that he didn't rot there.

"The reason I called you boys here this morning is because we have to do something about this small problem we have," Gerry explained.

"You guys have to go back there in the woods and do what you have to do to take care of this. I can't do all of this by myself."

With much grumbling the "boys" prepared to return to the scene of the crime. They cursed their youngest brother with every step they took.

Fred carried a small spade and an axe in a belt pack. It was a relic of his National Guard days and the spade was known as an excavation tool used for digging foxholes. "Every neighbor we have is probably looking out their window right now, trying to figure out what we are doing," he grumbled to John and Barney.

It was not likely any of the neighbors would be energetic enough to follow them through the woods. With the constant drizzle now common in the fall months, it was another good day to prop their feet upon their own stove's fender and read a good book.

It took about half an hour of steady walking to reach the place the men sought. They had passed the place where Adam had shot and killed the young man awhile back down the trail. The constant rain had finally washed the bloody leaves on down into the small nearby stream, but they knew the exact spot where he had fallen and died.

"If those guys had walked another 15 minutes in this direction, all our gooses would have been cooked," Fred said to his brothers. "One of us should have killed Adam a long time ago. Boy is he stupid. Sitting there on his ass before the fire, smoking a cigarette and drinking his first cup of coffee, letting those guys just stroll on back here. I just cannot believe how stupid he is," John continued to grumble.

Locating the place they sought was an easy matter. They had almost grown up in these woods and had hunted deer all over this area of their uncle's farm their entire lives. When they were poor, before their father acquired his Midas touch, deer meat was a staple on their dinner table. Their mother could cook deer meat a hundred different ways.

It was lucky they had come back here they discovered. "Look at that Fred," John said. "Most of the old brush we piled down into that old well has rotted and fallen down inside."

The boys began digging in earnest. While John shoveled dirt and threw big stones down into the well, the other two men were busily chopping small trees and brush and piling it down inside the old well.

After a lot of digging and shoveling and chopping, the incredibly nasty job was finally complete. They spent quite some time there, raking the top evenly with a green bough of pine, placing some dead leaves over the disturbed ground and then placing some small limbs and brush over their handiwork.

"Now, we should be OK," Fred said. He was always the ring-leader and the boss of any project simply because he was the oldest and was much bigger and meaner than his brothers.

They returned to their mother's house and told her the chore had been completed. "Nobody will ever know anything is there," they bragged and they were almost correct.

Each of the boys then showered and put on clean clothing which they had brought with them for this purpose while their mother threw their muddy clothes in the washer and dryer. They could not return to their own homes in their muddy condition. Someone would be asking questions and the fewer questions they had to answer the better they all would be they agreed.

"If any of you ever open your mouths about what went on today, you will have to answer to me," Fred warned all of them.

Each of them shook their heads and promised never to speak of the day's events.

Chapter 4

Meanwhile Sheriff Schneider was conferring with the county prosecuting attorney about Adam and the charges against him.

"Why do you think he shot that guy," the Sheriff asked the prosecutor. "The dead boy's father said he watched Adam raise his rifle, aim it, and shoot his son. I can only think that he meant to kill him. I just cannot understand why he would do that. What does it mean," he wondered.

The PA said, "You don't think it was an accident? That he really was shooting at a deer as he claims?"

"No, I do not think he was hunting. Those boys just don't make mistakes like that. They have been hunting deer legally and illegally since they were big enough and strong enough to hold a gun steady. They know a deer when they see one. They are not known to be careless or to shoot at noises."

"That's kind of like Gerry claiming that body was her husband, Charlie. She has to know that with a different blood type than his, the body they found could not possibly be her husband, but she insists it is. She writes those damn letters to the editor of that scroungy newspaper asking for a coroner's inquest. That editor and the young woman writer drive me crazy asking me why that hasn't happened yet. I just don't know what to do or say anymore."

Prosecutor Matt Slevin sympathized with Sheriff Schneider, but said there wasn't a lot he could tell him.

"If you think Adam shot this other guy deliberately, and all that you have shown me so far points that way, then we can charge him with voluntary manslaughter. The judge or the jury may lower that to involuntary manslaughter, but I don't think we have quite enough evidence that we can actually charge him with murder. You just don't have enough proof other than the father's statement. Now if someone other than the father was in those woods that day and saw it, then we could go for murder one."

Sheriff Schneider knew there had not been anyone else in the woods that day because no one else had come forward and said so. In this county if someone saw something they told someone else, and so on down the line until it got back to him. So far, no one had come forward, so no one had seen it happen.

Determined to grill Adam all day and all night if he had to, Sheriff Schneider stomped back to his jail to pull Adam from his cell.

When he arrived, he found that Adam had a visitor, his mother, Gerry. "Damn that woman," he snapped, "She comes here every day to plot and plan with Adam. I'm gonna put a stop to that. If she would leave him alone, he might tell me something, but with her advising and plotting, he won't open his damn mouth."

As he entered his office he stomped into the visitor's area and said, "Gerry, I want you to stop coming by here every day. You are not doing your boy a bit of good and you may actually be hurting his case."

"Sheriff, I will continue to come here every day and visit with my son. I have that right. There is no rule posted anywhere that says I can't, so I'm gonna be here whether you like it or not. He likes his cigarettes so I bring him a pack every day and besides that he likes to talk to his Mama," she replied.

Slamming the door to the visitor's room, the now furious Sheriff Schneider, cursing the woman with every flaming cuss word he knew, went flying down the hall to the jailer's office.

"I want you to keep that woman away from Adam. I need to question him some more, see if you can get rid of her."

The jailer, one of the lowest paid and lowest energy personnel on the Sheriff's staff, went slouching down the hallway to the visitor's room. Opening the door with a bang, he said, "Visiting hours are over. You need to leave now." Gerry leaned her body forward and kissed her son's forehead through the large wire mesh as he pressed his forehead to the divider which separated them as she prepared to leave.

Gerry had no more than departed the interlocking doors to the outside when Adam was brought to the "interrogation room" for further questioning by the Sheriff and the local State Police troopers. The interrogation room was nothing more than the dining room of the Sheriff's residence which was attached to the jail. This was the "home" provided him by the county as part of his salary.

But Adam knew they didn't have a clue what had happened and he refused to say one word no matter what they asked. He even refused to give his full name. No way would he help them. Let them build their case against him without any help from him, he smirked to himself.

Finally giving up in disgust, the Sheriff yelled for the jailer to replace Adam in his cell. "And keep his cigarettes away from him. Just give him one with each meal and one before he goes to bed. That way his mother won't need to visit him every day and bring him more," he snarled.

Chapter 5

After months of waiting, a trial date was finally set to hear the evidence against Adam. Mr. Rogerson had appealed to the court for a change of venue saying he could not get an unbiased jury in Green County but Judge Stearn had ruled against him, saying that little piddle-assed local newspaper couldn't influence anyone.

Little did Judge Stearn know the preparations George had made to cover the trial. For once in his life, he had sobered up long enough to hire an out-of- town hotshot reporter to cover the events and had even gone so far as to hire a courtroom artist to make sketches. He was ready. This was going to be one of the biggest events in the history of Green County, George was convinced. News media from all across the country had been calling him for information about the shooting and the fire and the man found in the fire. Bring on the judge, George smiled to himself.

Day one of the trial saw Adam brought to the courtroom looking spiffy in a black dress suit, powder blue shirt and darker blue printed tie and shiny slippers. His always unruly black curly hair had been styled and cut by an expert. The only things marring his good looks that day were the handcuffs which held his hands before him.

Judge Stearn admonished the jailer for having him cuffed when he was brought before the prospective jurors. "From now on, take them damn cuffs off before he comes through my door," he scolded.

The judge did not want to leave any item overlooked that could result in a mistrial or later have himself be accused by some smart-assed attorney of making errors. So from that day on, Adam walked into the courtroom with a swagger and a serious look on his handsome face.

There were 50 prospective jurors seated around the room. They had supposedly been randomly selected by a jury committee of two from the registered voter lists. Random did not actually apply in this particular case because, unknown to the judge, the selection committee actually had previously sorted the prospective juror list. If they pulled a name from the list that they knew was old or decrepit or just plain stupid, or it was someone they simply didn't like, they merely threw that name out and drew another. There were hundreds more available if need be, but Judge Stearn was confident he could find 14 people to sit in judgment of Adam. He needed 12 jurors and 2 alternates then the trial could begin.

The first twelve prospective jurors were seated in special high-back leather chairs placed inside the court box facing the judge. These seven women and five men, all white, where chosen because their juror number order was 1 through 12.

The judge began questioning the first 12 prospective jurors by asking if there were any seated who could not serve because they knew the defendant. All knew of him, but only two admitted to being on speaking terms with him. Those two were dismissed so jurors numbered 13 and 14 were then called to be seated in their place.

The judge continued until all twelve seats and two alternate seats were filled. He then turned the questioning over to the prosecutor who had first choice for questioning and bumping rights.

The prosecutor, who sat on the right side of the courtroom on the judge's left side and facing the defense attorney's table across the way, asked if anyone seated wanted to be excused because of age or sickness or problems at home and lost a couple of them and the next two in line were then seated. The PA used one of his three permitted bumps without reason to remove one woman who had been eyeing the defendant rather closely with a smile on her face. He did not have to give a reason for these three bumps, but just had to say, bump him or her.

He chose one man because of his strong demeanor. The judge would never know it, but the PA had known this young man personally for a very long time and at one time the man had owed him some money which he had eventually repaid. It would be nice to have him on the jury, so he kept him.

Finally, he had no options left for bumping, so he sat down.

Judge Stearn advised the defendant's lawyer, the same Mr. Rogerson he had dealt with earlier in the insurance case for the young man's mother, and who was now also volunteering to represent the defendant free of charge, to utilize his options. He could either accept the present jury or he could make his bumps and changes.

The defense attorney, seated to the Judge's right and directly facing the PA's table across the room, could also bump freely without cause three times. The first person he removed was the man who had owed the prosecutor money at one time. He had noticed the glances they exchanged and knew something was askew.

Rogerson wanted as many younger women as he could get for the jury. He realized that his handsome client would hold a special appeal to every woman from 18-50.

Finally, two days after jury selection had begun, there were 12 jurors and two alternates seated in the high-backed leather chairs. Adam's fate rested on their decision.

Attorney Rogerson felt good about the juror prospects. There were now eight women on the jury, all white since there was not one black nor Hispanic family in the county at that time, all between the ages of 28-47 and four men, all white, under 40 years of age. This lack of ethnic jurors was not deliberate. There just were so few ethnic people in the county as a whole that this had just quite naturally occurred. Not many outsiders wanted to live there anyway. The alternates included one other young woman and a very old man. Yes, he was happy with his jury.

The opening salvo was fired by prosecutor Matt Slevin. Testifying first would be the father of the deceased.

"Please raise your right hand, state your name, and do you swear to tell the truth, the whole truth and nothing but the truth, so help you God," the bailiff asked him as he held a Bible out to the victim's father to swear upon.

"My name is John Smith. I am the father of the deceased, Michael Smith. I do swear to tell the truth, the whole truth and nothing but the truth, so help me God," the father said, then he sat down.

"Do you see the man in this courtroom whom you saw shoot your son," he was asked.

"Yes."

"Please point him out to the jurors," the father was instructed.

"It was that man sitting right over there, the one you call the defendant, who shot my son. I saw him do it," he cried.

The judge made a note to the clerk to indicate for the record that the father was pointing at Adam.

"Did you see him take aim and fire his gun at your son?"

"Yes, I did. He was behind a tree and I saw him raise the gun, point it at my son, and pull the trigger. He was wearing a heavy brown coat, hunter orange on his vest and work boots. He killed my son."

"Do you think the defendant deliberately murdered your son?" "Yes, I do."

Objections were heard from the defendant's attorney. "You are asking this man to make an assumption," he told the judge.

The judge instructed the jury to disregard the dead man's father's statement.

"Why would he deliberately kill your son?" "Objection," Mr. Rogerson yelled. "Sustained."

"I'm sorry, your honor," the PA said. "Did either you or your son know this man?"

"No, I had never seen him before that day and as far as I know my son didn't know him either," the grief-stricken father replied.

"Did you know you were on their private property when you went hunting that day?"

"No, I did not. My son had arranged the hunt some weeks prior and we thought we were on an adjoining neighbor's land. We did not know we had wandered off their land and were on the neighboring property until after that man killed my son," the father said.

"Objection," Mr. Rogerson said.

"Strike that last sentence of his statement," Judge Stearn told the jury. "Did you hear or see anyone else in the woods that day who could have shot your son. Maybe it wasn't the defendant?" the prosecutor queried. "No, there had not been anyone else around us all day."

"Do you know if the defendant saw you that day?"

"Objection, this calls for a conclusion of the witness," Mr. Rogerson said. "Sustained."

"No, I don't believe he did or I would be dead too," the grieving father replied.

"Objection."

"Sustained. Please instruct your witness to answer only what he is asked," the judge instructed the PA.

"And, you saw this man very deliberately pull his gun up, aim it at your son, and fire it at him?"

"Yes."

"Do you think he meant to kill him?" "Yes."

"Objection."

"Sustained. The jury will disregard that last statement." "No further questions, your honor," Mr. Slevin said.

"Mr. Rogerson, you may now question this witness," the Judge instructed. "Now, Mr. Smith, why on earth do you think my client deliberately shot your son?"

"I don't know why. I just know he did."

"They did not know one another and you had never seen him before. You got only a brief glance at him when you say you saw him hidden behind a tree, yet you can readily identify him sitting across the room from you now.

"How many times have you seen this man before today?"

"Twice. I saw him behind that tree and I saw him when he came back into the woods to help us."

"When he came back into the woods the second time, was he wearing the same clothing he had been wearing when he allegedly shot your son?"

"No, he had changed clothes."

"How long had it taken him to leave the area, change his clothing, and get back to you to give aid?"

"About 15 minutes."

"How far away from you was he when he fired the shot that killed your son?"

"About 300 yards."

"That's a long way to see details of a man's face, hair, clothing, etc. Could you be wrong in your identification of the shooter?"

"No, I couldn't. He shot my son."

"Judge, please instruct this witness to answer only those questions I ask him without adding his thoughts."

"Answer only those questions you are asked," he instructed the witness. "The jury will disregard the last part of the witness's statement."

"Now, Mr. Smith, I have reason to doubt your ability to identify this man sitting here before me. I'm not saying you are lying, I'm just saying I think you could be mistaken. This young man sitting here has never been in serious trouble before this.

"He didn't know your son as far as you know and they had never had words. "It was approximately a quarter mile from where your wounded son lay dying to this young man's home. He would have had to have been running pretty fast to leave the tree, run home, change clothing from the boots on up, and run back to you to assist you.

"Do you really feel he could have done all this in as little as 15 minutes?" "Well, he is young and strong. I don't see why he couldn't have done it that quick."

"No further questions, your honor," Mr. Slevin said.

Judge Stearn told Mr. Smith to step down. "Call your next witness," he told the prosecutor.

What followed was a boring presentation by the investigating officer, the coroner, and others involved in the investigation.

Murder, Relatively Speaking

Finally, the prosecutor said, "I rest my case, your honor."
"Thank you. Mr. Rogerson, you may call your first witness."
"I wish to call Mrs. Geraldine Jones," Mr. Rogerson said.

Adam's mother shambled up to the witness chair, raised her right hand, spoke her full name and swore to tell the truth, the whole truth and nothing but the truth as she laid her hand on the Bible held toward her by the bailiff.

"Now Mrs. Jones, was your son, Adam, at your house on the day the other young man was accidentally shot and killed?"

"Yes."

"Was he there to go hunting on the property?" "No."

"What was he there for then. You have just heard the father of the   deceased say that he saw your son, dressed in hunter's orange, standing behind a tree and shooting his son. Was this possible? Why was he at your house?" "That man, pointing to the father, may have seen someone shoot his son, but it was not my son. Adam was at home with me and his brothers. They were going to split and stack some firewood that had been delivered for me. He was not hunting.

"Why then did he go into the woods with his brother to help the dying man?" "A man with a gun ran by our house and shouted that someone had gotten shot in the woods, and he was going for the doctor. He asked if we could go back and help the wounded man. Adam said he would go. One of the brothers went with him."

51

"Was the fleeing man running by your house dressed in hunter orange or have on any other orange item as part of his clothing?"

"Yes, he did. He had on an old gray work shirt under a faded green sweatshirt and had a stocking cap on his head and was also wearing an orange vest of some type. He wore work boots.

He appeared to be about six foot, four inches tall and weighed maybe 250 pounds."

"Your sons went running back into the woods immediately after the other guy had run by your house saying he was going for a doctor?"

"Yes."

"So it could not have been your son this poor grieving father saw that morning but someone other than your son. Perhaps it was the man you saw running by your house going for the doctor?"

"Yes, but it wasn't Adam. He was at home with me and his brothers." "What type of clothing did Adam have on?"

"He was wearing denim pants, a blue plaid quilted shirt, high top work boots and a knitted cap on his head," Gerry said as she described her son. "He is five feet, eleven inches tall and weighs about 180 pounds."

"No further questions."

Prosecutor Slevin was working up to discrediting the mother but got absolutely nowhere with her. Never once did her story vary from the original telling. Her son was innocent.

"Call your next witness Mr. Rogerson," the judge advised. "I call the defendant, Adam Jones to the stand," he said.

Everyone in the room drew in breath. This was an unexpected turn of events. No one expected Adam to be placed on the stand.

"Were you in the woods behind your mother's house the day Mr. Smith's son was shot and killed," Rogerson asked him.

"Yes."

"What? This court just heard your mother say you were not back in those woods hunting that day so you could not have killed the man."

"That's right. I wasn't back in the woods hunting. I was there to help that wounded man. You see, there was this man who went running by our house yelling for help, saying he was going for a doctor. Said someone back in the woods had been shot and needed help. Me and my brother Fred ran back to see what we could do. So you see, Judge, I was in those woods that day."

Mr. Rogerson smiled. This was going better than he would have thought possible. Adam made a very convincing witness.

He was well-read, articulate and handsome. Anyone with a lick of sense would believe him.

After three days of testimony, Judge Stearn said the magical words that would turn the work over to the jury.

He admonished them about not talking about the case to any outsiders, and explained they could not call anyone or read a newspaper while they were deliberating.

"You can bring back one of three possible decisions," he instructed them. "You can find the defendant guilty as charged with voluntary manslaughter.

That means he did it and went to the woods with the express purpose of doing harm, not necessarily to this man in particular, but to someone.

"You can find him guilty to the lesser charge of involuntary manslaughter.

That means he did it accidentally without premeditation.

"Or, the third decision could be Not Guilty. He is not guilty of any crime.

Someone else may have shot this man but not Mr. Adam Jones.

"The decision is yours to make and it must be unanimous. Are there any questions?" No questions were asked and Judge Stearn motioned for the bailiff to lead them into the jury room and advised the defense attorney and prosecutor to leave a number where they could be found when a verdict was reached. Everyone involved in the investigation of this crime was astonished when just two hours after it convened, the jury sent word they had reached a verdict. At 7 p.m. the prosecutor, the defendant with his mother and his attorney, and the defendant's brothers filed back into the courtroom to hear the jury's verdict read.

"Has the jury reached a verdict?" the Judge asked once they were all again seated.

"We have your honor," the forewoman answered.

"Would the forewoman please stand and read the verdict? Mr. Jones, you may rise and face the jury," he told Adam.

Adam, along with his attorney, stood and faced the twelve jurors. Adam was nervous but Rogerson felt pretty confidant.

His job had not been really difficult. He felt he had planted a seed of doubt in the minds of the jurors with the story of the man running by the house going for the doctor.

"The forewoman may now proceed," Judge Stearn said. "How say ye?"

"We, the jury in the aforementioned case *State versus Adam Jones*, find the defendant Not Guilty," the forewoman said.

Adam gasped, his mother fainted dead away, and his brothers gave a loud whoop. The father of the dead man dropped his head to the table and cried. "Case dismissed," Judge Stearn said as he struck his gavel on the desk, gathered his robes around himself and left the courtroom.

Adam was once again a free man.

Chapter 6

Finally, something good has happened to me," Gerry thought to herself after she came to her senses after fainting in the courtroom.

She was surprised to see her sons and attorney Rogerson sitting around looking on as the emergency medical technicians worked over her in their attempt to revive her.

"I'm sorry," she said.

"That's OK mom," Fred said. "It was pretty exciting for all of us."

The emergency personnel, seeing that she was now okay, packed up their gear and hightailed it out of the courtroom. Fred helped his mom to her feet and with a son on each side of her she was escorted to their car. Rogerson followed the entourage to the parking lot where, after shaking hands with each of them, he got into his car and drove away.

Adam was still pretty shaky but the others were in a party mood. "Let's hit the liquor store for a bottle and head to my house," Fred said.

His mother was not a drinker because of her diabetes, but she might be tempted to take just a small sip today to celebrate their victory.

After stopping at the liquor store for a bottle of Calvert's and a 12 pack of Cokes, they took the short drive out to Fred's house for the celebration.

"Fix me just a small one," Gerry said.

Fred, knowing his mom's almost non-existent tolerance for alcohol fixed her a pretty stiff drink. He needed to talk to his brothers alone, but she would never allow that. She wanted to know every little detail of their lives. It was a chore to keep anything from her.

Feeling in a party mood, Gerry tipped the glass up and polished her drink off in three loud gulps.

It hit her stomach like a ton of rocks and within fifteen minutes she could be heard gently snoring on the couch. Fred placed a small pillow under her head, covered her with a crocheted afghan, and left her there before returning to the kitchen for a heart-to-heart talk with his brothers.

"Well we have gotten that out of the way," he began.

"The big fight is now before us and we have to win that one too. I know Mom is the beneficiary of the insurance money Dad carried, but we all know that we will get a large share of it. We just have to make sure she gets it. Any ideas from you guys?" he queried.

"Well we have given them Dad's wallet. It was pretty ingenious to fix it the way it had to be fixed. Those dumb bastards will never know the military ID was altered," Barney said.

Always the artistic one of the four, it had been Barney's job to do the alteration and he had done a very good job he thought.

"Placing his ring in the ashes at the garage after the fire had cooled was a nice touch, too," John said.

"Why didn't you place the one he always wore in the ashes," he was asked. "Are you kidding? And have that thing damaged by the flames? Are you crazy? That ring is worth a fortune and I'm gonna save it for my son when he gets older. Everyone will have forgotten about the fire by the time he grows up," Fred said.

"Now we all have to rally around Mom and see that she does as we tell her," Fred continued. "I know I will be seeing a lot of her so I can keep her in line." While the brothers continued their plotting, the local Green County Banner newspaper was busily preparing to put out a special edition with more huge dark headlines.

"Adam Innocent," it proclaimed across the top of the front page in 72 point bold type.

After a long verbose story written by the newly acquired hotshot reporter, there was a picture of a sobbing father, grieving for his dead son after the Not Guilty verdict was rendered.

The caption under his picture quoted him saying, "They got away with murder." And there were many in the county who believed they had.

Another picture showed the mother of the accused killer stretched out on the floor of the courtroom being worked on by the EMTs, this too, as a result of the Not Guilty verdict.

By this time there were few living in Green County who still felt sorry for Gerry. Most of the readers of the newspaper figured that somewhere along the road in raising her handsome sons, the mother surely had gone wrong somewhere. They were out of control.

Chapter 7

The hotshot writer for the Green County Banner was ready to move on. He was in the big time now. Hadn't he successfully reported on one of the biggest stories of his career? With that experience behind him he could begin to name his own price, so with that thought in mind he headed back up to the Windy City.

Stepping in to fill his shoes now was a young, very inexperienced woman who had absolutely no writing experience except for obituaries, but a determination to acquire some.

With the big court case behind him, and with another staff member waiting to go on her honeymoon, it had been time for George to add someone else to his staff. He had been very impressed with the resume handed him by this very eager future writer.

Upon learning she had experience on an electronic typesetting machine, he hired her on the spot since his newspaper was still being prepared the old-fashioned way, typeset on a Linotype machine and printed on a flatbed press with each sheet of paper fed into the machine by hand. A bonus for George was the fact she could type accurately about 150 words per minute. She would be a godsend to his small operation.

Sallianne was not yet 30 years old with two young sons, a husband and a lot of office experience behind her. She was experienced in bookkeeping, customer service, typesetting and many other areas including having worked for a couple of years as a computer programmer, a rather new line of work but one that would become more important to this small weekly newspaper as the years wore on. Fitting nicely into his lean staff, Sallianne was asked to start work the day after her interview.

Starting out handling subscription renewals, manning the telephones, and writing the obituaries was a good learning process. She was totally honest and George had no fear that she would take off with the money she brought in with the ads and subscriptions she sold. Besides all that the readers loved her and it would take a load off George's back and add to his prestige to be able to say he had one reporter.

Sallianne had not written a story since she was in high school speech class and had worked on the high school newspaper and annual staff. She had no other journalistic training of any kind. She was a good speller, a fast reader and worked with the public very well and they trusted her from the start. She was possessed with an avid enthusiasm for writing and soon moved into re-writing the local community news that was handed in by the area correspondents. She was so successful in re-writing copy from these half-dozen correspondents that the once ugly feature was now a hit with his readers.

The correspondents no longer merely told who Mr. and Mrs. So and So visited last week, they also gave the purpose of the visit, what was fixed for dinner and their relationship to others in the tiny communities scattered around Green County. If the correspondent found one of her friends sick, she printed a prayer for their recovery. If they were canning vegetables, she might give a favorite recipe she had collected. Sometimes a child or grandchild would be celebrating a birthday when she visited so she would run a picture she had taken with the community news. All these ideas added interest to the once uncaring readers of the newspaper.

The only problem was George could not keep her busy enough to occupy all her time. She was becoming bored, so she instigated a column where anyone could call in and leave a gripe or make a comment. No names could be mentioned unless the person leaving the gripe was speaking about an elected official; they were fair game and could be identified. This was not exactly like a gossip column, but "Say Your Thing" certainly was close to being one and it was another very popular feature in the paper, sometimes running on to two or more pages. She encouraged readers to write letters to the editor either to thank someone for a favor or just to vent their anger toward someone or some event, so the op-ed page was always fun to read.

Always a frantic worker, she could do the work of three other staffers. George decided to ask her to do some interviewing and story writing to help fill out her days at the office. What a brilliant idea this turned out to be. He had finally struck gold. Sallianne Carmichael had arrived.

Every person Sallianne interviewed gave George glowing remarks about her work and her accuracy. They were not afraid to tell her the most intimate details of their lives. Soon anyone wanting to see his name in print was calling

George and asking him to let Sallianne interview them, so he turned her loose on the public and hired another young woman to fill the void she left in the office when she was out on an assignment.

She quickly started turning in massive stories and pictures that captured the essence of those she interviewed. Subscriptions and news stand sales skyrocketed.

It wasn't long before those incarcerated in the local jail were writing her letters, asking her to write their story about how they had been wrongly jailed. Some of those in jail had had a turnaround in their lives and wanted to give tips to the public on how to avoid being hit by a burglar or to tell their experiences while on drugs. While she was inexperienced, she did do some of those stories, but she quickly realized that her forte was interviewing and writing down-to- earth human interest stories.

One person who repeatedly came into the office to see her and ask her to write their story was Gerry Jones. She was ready to talk to someone, she told Sallianne and she wanted to talk to no one other than her.

"But I don't have the experience yet to write your story," she told Gerry. "Why does it have to be me who writes it?"

"Because I trust you to write the truth," she told Sallianne many times. Sallianne discussed the idea of writing Gerry's life story with her boss.

George was dubious about this assignment. "It will be a very tough job," he told her.

"I know, that is why I have kept putting her off. I just don't feel capable of doing that big a story yet."

George thought it over and finally decided, "No, you are wrong. You are just the one to do her story. I want you to take her to lunch at a nice restaurant, buy her a drink or two, and interview her. I will help you write the story later if you need help," he said.

"The trial against the insurance company is coming up very soon. I think this would be an ideal time for you to tell her story. If she wants you to do it, try to get an exclusive if you can," he advised.

He planned to run Gerry's life story just before that insurance trial began and mention that it was about to begin as part of her life story to build up interest, and, of course, to sell more newspapers.

So with some trepidation, Sallianne agreed to do this interview. It was a story every reporter worth his salt would love to do but Gerry would not give it to anyone except her. She also wouldn't let anyone other than Sallianne take her picture. What a coup this was for the bright young maybe someday reporter. All the arrangements were made for the interview to take place a week later. The restaurant was chosen by Sallianne and sample questions were provided by George. This was just in case Sallianne had trouble coming up with some on her own, but he need not have worried. She had plenty of questions she wanted to ask. Sallianne had been intrigued with the mystery since the day it had happened and long before she had begun working at the newspaper. She had all kinds of ideas of how it happened, who did it and why. It would be many years later before she would learn the whole truth, but for right now, she felt prepared to do the biggest story of her life.

On Tuesday of the following week and driving her gloriously yellow Jeep, Sallianne picked Gerry up at her house and drove to a nearby city to the quiet restaurant she had chosen. She told Gerry to order whatever she wanted for lunch and offered to buy drinks.

"What would you like to drink, Gerry?" she asked.

"I really do not want anything. If I try to drink alcohol it sends my sugar levels sky high and I might have to go back to the hospital to get it leveled out," she told Sallianne.

So they enjoyed a nice quiet lunch and both drank sweetened iced tea. Sallianne was not a drinker either so she was very happy that no alcohol would be served.

Once the lunch was finished, they leisurely drove back into Green County to a nice large state park that had picnic tables.

The sun was shining brightly on this warm fall day and the weather was nearly perfect. In the distance the leaves were turning nicely and it was a very peaceful spot to have their interview.

Sallianne arrayed her notebooks and pens in front of her and popped the lid from a couple of diet drinks, handing one to Gerry.

"OK, Gerry, are you ready to begin?" she asked. "Yes, I am," she replied.

"You have maintained all along that your husband was dead and you buried him in the graveyard on the outside of town, the same grave that was exhumed a few years ago. Is that correct?"

"Yes."

"What makes you say it was your husband in that first fire? All the forensic evidence says it wasn't Charlie in that fire. What makes you so sure it was?"

"I know my husband is dead. If Charlie was alive, he would have made contact with his boys, by now. That's how I know he is dead."

By now, many years had gone by since the fire occurred that killed the man she claimed was her husband but police investigators were no closer to a solution than they had been the night of the fire.

Some people reported to the police that they had seen Charlie sneaking into her house or hiding from them in a hollow next to the house, others reported they had seen him in various cities, but none of these claims could be substantiated.

Others reported to the police that they had heard Charlie speaking to her. Charlie's sister lived next door to where Gerry was now living and reported she was out walking in her yard one day when the arthritis in her feet made her have to sit down on the lawn and rest. She said during an interview earlier in the case with Sallianne that she heard Gerry speaking to someone through an open window nearby, but the man's voice definitely did not belong to her brother, Charlie.

"You can go for years not hearing a loved one's voice, but when you do hear it again, you still know if it is your relative," the sister-in-law averred.

The state police had even staked out Gerry's house from a nearby hillside with the hopes of serving the murder warrant on Charlie if he should show himself. That effort failed when a very mean dog that Gerry usually kept chained with a log chain to her back porch post got lose and came toward the police. Rather than their shooting the dog and alerting someone to their surveillance, they left quickly. The dog was mean and vicious, Sallianne knew. She had seen where the log chain holding it to the porch had scraped the threshold of the door down a couple of inches when it had been let inside the house with the chain still attached

The police would never reveal what their motive had been for not just walking up to the front door of Gerry's house and searching it for Charlie since they had a valid arrest warrant. Perhaps they had a legitimate reason for not approaching Gerry's house, but if so, it was never made public.

But that made no impression on Gerry. She insisted many times during that five-hour mountain top interview that the dead man found in the fire was her husband, Charlie. Nothing Sallianne asked or said could make her change her story.

Gerry related how she had been visiting at Fred's house the night of the fire and said she had been to the local fish stand in a nearby town to buy fish sandwiches for their supper. This was a common occurrence. Everyone in the neighborhood went to this same fish stand when they wanted a good fish sandwich. The catfish were caught fresh every day in the nearby river and served up at this little restaurant. She said she was going to take the sandwiches home for her and Charlie's supper after she had concluded her visit with Fred. Gerry said she had been at Fred's house when she was notified of the fire, giving the impression to everyone who had asked, that she had not been home once already before she was notified at Fred's place of the fire.

Sallianne was quick to realize that Gerry was telling a whopper of a lie. She had already been home and had left the fish sandwiches on the kitchen table for Charlie to eat for his supper when he got the leaves raked.

Hadn't Charlie's cousin Jim, told the police that Charlie had offered him a fish sandwich? Didn't anyone else ever doubt her statement? The statement struck Sallianne right in the face.

What was true and what was a lie in all the stories Gerry related to Sallianne that afternoon?

As Sallianne slowly drove Gerry home that closing afternoon, she asked Gerry about her rags to riches then back to rags story. After all, she had been raised in a fairly poor family, then she had married Charlie of the Midas touch. She had gone from being poor to being rich, then back to being poor again as Charlie's stars fell. It was obvious to all that Gerry liked being rich much better. "I hate being poor," Gerry admitted. "I think that awful insurance company should just send me my money."

"Well, when you get that trial behind you, maybe they will," Sallianne soothed her.

Murder, Relatively Speaking

That trial was coming up very soon and George was now anxious to get this story into the paper so he could concentrate on getting his hotshot reporter back along with the courtroom artist. That would be a blockbuster for sure.

But as Gerry was being dropped at her home Sallianne asked her if she had ever considered writing a book about all her troubles and her road from rags to riches and back to rags.

"I'm not very good with words. Maybe someday when I get my money and am rich, you and I can write a book together and I'll tell you the truth," Gerry said.

Sallianne, who had planned to drive straight home, decided at this point she had to return to her office and discuss this new problem with George.

"I know she was lying the whole afternoon," she told George. I must have asked her at least a half dozen times how she knew for certain her husband was dead. Her most often repeated reason for knowing he was dead was to say to me, "Because I know my husband is dead."

How did she know he was dead? The man exhumed from her husband's grave was not her Charlie. No one knew who that man was and not too many cared who it was. How did she know Charlie was dead? It was true that no one had for sure ever seen him alive after the night of the fire. But on the other hand, no one had ever seen him dead either. Which was it? Dead, or alive? This statement, "I know my husband is dead" would return many times over the next few months to haunt Sallianne. It was the one statement she could not reconcile with what she knew about the case from the forensic reports.

George insisted she write her story as though what Gerry had told her was the truth. It went against every instinct she possessed and it influenced the story she wrote. But Gerry was happy with it and she got a lot of compliments, but Sallianne was not happy writing up what she considered was a pack of lies. Sallianne felt that the only way Gerry could possibly know her husband was dead was if she had personal knowledge of that event herself. "Was that possible?" she asked herself. "Did this little old lady have something to do with her husband's death? Did she kill him to collect his insurance money? If she did, what was her motive other than collecting his insurance money? Has she ever been a suspect in his disappearance?"

No answers were to be found but it gave Sallianne a great deal to think about.

Chapter 8

A month or so after Gerry's life story ran in the local weekly newspaper, her trial against the insurance company began and it was a nearly open and shut case.

Even without the star witness for the insurance company, Edward Morris, the case was easily decided; Gerry would not collect that cool two million dollars.

Mr. Morris had been paid a pretty hefty sum in advance along with various other witnesses to appear and bolster the case against Gerry's claim, but he did not appear to speak in the courtroom. The headline in the Green County Banner read, "Edward Morris, where are you?"

Edward Morris would never be heard from nor seen again.

The trial lasted less than one week. Charlie was not dead, the jury said. It had not been his body that was found in the fire but rather an unknown person who would never be positively identified. In fact, the same court had long ago ruled that Charlie was guilty of murder and was a fugitive from justice. It was believed at first that Charlie was trying to defraud the insurance company by planting the unknown man's body in his garage and then setting fire to it. And according to law one cannot benefit from committing murder so no one would get this money.

Gerry would never be a rich woman. She and her boys were devastated.

Chapter 9

In the coming months Gerry would ask for Sallianne's help many times. She had come into her office many years prior to the insurance lawsuit being settled and very sadly asked Sallianne, "Would you be my friend?"

Sallianne had no reason not to be friendly with Gerry so she agreed.

Gerry knew nearly everything that could be known about Sallianne including the fact that she was so honest, so using that factor alone Gerry felt no compunction about asking Sallianne to type some papers for her.

Sallianne agreed to do the work and would never charge Gerry for the work knowing that she had no money with which to pay her anyway.

There were several times when Gerry brought several pages of hand written notes to Sallianne to be typed on special paper which she would provide. There might be eight or ten legal sized pages of penciled notes to type up. Sallianne was required to put in capital letters to start a sentence and a period where it was needed to end one since there was not one punctuation mark in the entire document. Each document was the same, only one capital letter to lead off the first page and then not another mark. Gerry asked Sallianne not to make any carbon copies, and not suspecting she would ever regret doing so, Sallianne readily agreed.

All the papers she typed for Gerry were addressed to the U. S. Patent office and dealt with new designs for cars or their engines. Sallianne knew that Gerry couldn't change a flat tire on her car much less design a new type of car so she asked Gerry who was doing this design work.

Every one of the papers to the patent office was signed by GEM, International, by Gerry Jones, President.

Gerry replied that one of her boys had been living with her for awhile and to kill time he would sit at the kitchen table as she worked and write the information down as he thought of it.

She related that as he sat there writing, he was drinking beer. He loved Pabst Blue Ribbon beer so Gerry brought him a six-pack from the local carryout liquor store every evening on her way home from work. Everyone who knew Gerry knew that she loved to spoil her sons, so she spent hundreds of dollars over the years buying that six-pack of Pabst every afternoon.

Gerry still had a part-time job, as many of the other single women in the area had, of helping stock the local grocery store and baking pies for their deli service. It was not much of a job and the pay was not large, but it made it possible for Gerry to stretch her small welfare check.

The carryout's proprietor would later report to the police that Gerry was an alcoholic and bought a six-pack of Pabst Blue Ribbon Beer to take home every night.

Chapter 10

By now ten years had gone by and the mystery of poor Charlie who either did die or did not die in a fire at his garage was still a hot topic around the local bar.

Sallianne had stayed busy with her work at the newspaper and had been promoted so many times by George that she was now in charge of the entire newspaper.

George was a great believer in educating and keeping the skills of his employees current, so he made arrangements to send Sallianne to Washington,

D. C. to attend a week's training conference so she had been making preparations to be away from home for a week.

Her plane was to leave the next Sunday morning on a cold day in November.

She traveled up the road past Gerry's old ramshackle house going to town to do some clothes shopping. Her husband was driving and her youngest son was in the back seat. As they traveled, they talked and jabbered, catching up on the news of the week.

As they came upon the area where Gerry's house had been located, they saw a lot of smoke and many fire apparatuses parked there.

"Please stop," she begged her husband.

Her husband, Martin, applied the brakes and asked if she was sure she wanted to stop. "You know how afraid of fire you are," he reminded her.

"Yes, I know, but I must stop and make sure Gerry is all right."

A long-time friend of hers walked up to her vehicle and asked that she not go any further. "It is not good," he advised Sallianne. "They have found two bodies in the ashes already. They may find others," he said.

"But is Gerry OK," Sallianne asked her friend.

"I'm sorry, but I'm afraid not. The first body they found was a female. The police believe it is Gerry," she was told.

Sallianne burst into a torrent of tears as she grieved for her one-time friend.

"Who else did they find if there were two bodies in the fire?" she asked her friend.

"They are not sure but they said it looked like a man's body and that he appeared to be about 42 years old."

"You have to remember that fires do terrible things to a human body so the male body will have to be identified by a pathologist. Based on the scraps of clothing on the woman's remains, it is consistent with being Gerry, but she too will be autopsied."

Martin urged Sallianne to leave the fire scene and return home with him. "You are much to upset to go shopping now," he said to her.

"No, I must get my shopping done. Let's go ahead and meet my friend and you two can return home. I will be home later on today."

"All right, but I think you should just come on home with me now," Martin said, but he continued to drive her to the friend's house who was going to help her shop since Sallianne had no sense of clothes style or colors at all.

Sallianne cried softly off and on for most of the afternoon as she and her friend completed her shopping.

The next morning after the fire on Sunday she went into George's office and asked him what he was going to write about the fire. Her friend at the fire scene had told her George had been there at the scene for all of Saturday night and most of the day on Sunday taking pictures and talking to fire and police officials.

"I'm not going to write a single word, but you are," George advised her. "This is your story. Go get it."

So saying, Sallianne loaded her camera, several pads of reporter's notebooks and some pens in her carryall and headed to the fire scene.

Officials were still milling around, discussing what had happened.

Charlie's brother was first on her list of interviews for that morning, so she headed across the street to Chad's home.

"Who do you think they are saying was found in that fire?" she asked Chad. "I don't know who it was but I can betcha they are saying it is Charlie they found," Chad said.

"That's right. I called the pathologist before leaving my office and a staff member told me that the male body removed from this fire belonged to Charlie and said he had died of smoke inhalation."

"I knew they would say that. They are wanting this case to be over and it is not over. Now it probably will never be over," Chad said.

Sallianne reminded Chad of all the times Charlie had been "seen" living in Gerry's place.

"Charlie was not living or visiting over there. I would have seen him the same as anybody else or he would have come over here to see me at some time in the last ten years," Chad said.

"Lordy, I just remembered, it was nearly ten years ago to this day when Charlie disappeared after that other fire."

Now, here it was ten years down the road, and another fire had just occurred at the Jones residence. In this fire, the authorities had found two more burned bodies, one was almost immediately identified as that of Gerry Jones and the second was most likely Charlie's.

He was right Sallianne realized. Almost exactly ten years ago today the mystery had begun.

After getting what little personal information she could from Chad to be used in the obituaries for the couple, Sallianne returned to her office to begin the heart-breaking chore of writing about her friend, Gerry. She had never met good old Charlie, so her sadness was caused mainly by the loss of Gerry.

Gerry's obituary was the easiest part of the story to write about, so she started with that to allow a little more time for her mind to settle. She knew George was nearly chomping at the bit waiting for her first reports regarding the fire so his re-writes could begin.

The first thing to do was to call the forensic pathologist once again and get the cause of death and find out whether or not positive identifications had been made on the bodies.

She was told by a shame-faced sounding pathologist that the bodies were indeed those of Charlie and Gerry Jones. Both had died of smoke inhalation meaning both were alive when the fire started because there was ash and soot found in the throats and lungs of both bodies.

"How can that be," Sallianne asked Dr. Parker. "You said the man who died in the first fire was Charlie, now you are saying this man is Charlie. I do not understand."

"I simply made a mistake when I identified the first fire victim," Dr. Parker explained to Sallianne.

"Well, are you sure it was Charlie this time? A friend at the fire yesterday told me the police thought the male body belonged to someone about 42 years of age and Charlie would be about 65 by now."

"I don't know who said that yesterday at the fire, but I am saying right now that this was a 65-year-old-man and that it is Charlie," Dr. Parker emphasized. Dr. Parker added that both bodies also contained a high concentration of alcohol. They were so drunk, especially Gerry whose blood alcohol content (BAC) was .385, that she would have been comatose when the fire started, he explained. Charlie's was just slightly less than hers.

Hanging up the telephone after talking with Dr. Parker, Sallianne then dialed the local fire chief to get a cause of the blaze and learned that the fire was indeed an act of arson.

"That fire had a good head of steam before anyone noticed it," she was told by fire chief Delbert King. "I have called in the state fire marshal and he is going to meet me there in an hour or so to begin his investigation, but I am positive an accelerant was used."

The fire marshal discovered that a substance, probably something much like turpentine, had been poured in a stream all throughout the inside of the house, both upstairs and down, and the fire was fed by that substance.

"We found a string of burn patterns all across the floor. It is likely that whoever set the fire was trapped inside the kitchen area before he could get out and was accidentally killed when he lit the match and ignited the fumes," the fire marshal said. "There would have been a massive buildup of fumes by the time this much accelerant was spread around and the match was lit. It would be what we in the business call a "flash-over," the fire marshal explained.

Sallianne's thoughts were going round and round as she tried to piece together all these forensic details.

Finally, about two hours after lunchtime which she could not eat, her stories were basically finished. It had been extremely difficult for her to put together the facts she was being given so quickly by so many experts, but she did the best she could, shooting her separate stories to George as each one was finished so he could begin the editing process.

Her stories would fill the entire front page along with a couple of the inside pages which were filled with sidebars, or related, stories and pictures. These stories were her one chance in a million to make a name for herself as a journalist, but Sallianne was absolutely exhausted when her job was done.

Sallianne had no more than stopped writing when the state police investigator and a local deputy sheriff arrived at her desk to question her about what she knew about the Jones family.

"We already know that you and Gerry were pretty good friends. We just want to know your take on this whole mess," the policeman said.

"I really do not know anything for sure about it. I had never met Charlie but Gerry asked me to be her friend and she also asked me to do some typing for her and I agreed to help her. That is about the extent of our friendship," she explained to the intimidating deputy who was doing most of the questioning. "Where are the copies you kept of the material you typed for her? Maybe there will be something there that will help us," he asked.

Sallianne replied that in respect for Gerry's request not to make a carbon copy, she had not done so, but explained the gist of the papers she had prepared. In hindsight, she would forever regret not keeping a copy of those papers in her private files, but with all that had been happening, that was now water under the bridge for her. She had no proof she had ever completed this work or even what it had been about.

The deputy saw that Sallianne was nearly at the end of her physical stamina and that he must not badger her any more today.

Before he left her office he commented, "I think you know more about this case than you are letting on. Maybe you don't even know what it is you know. Go on home and think about it awhile and get back to me. It could be dangerous for you to know something that the killer or killers can use against you."

So once the stories had all been given to George and he had been able to ask her relevant questions and do the editing of them successfully, and the police had gone, she wearily picked up her purse and left the office. She badly needed time alone to recover and rejuvenate herself, so she headed home to her bed. It might only be 4 p.m. but she had to lie down. Her body and mind could not take any more jabs or sorrow this day.

Lying there with the events and details of this tragedy swirling around madly inside her brain, she finally dozed off. Within minutes she was sitting upright in bed, scared to death.

Sallianne screamed for her husband to come to her. She was shaking so badly she could barely speak as she tried to explain to him the events and facts about the two fires that did not gel to her satisfaction.

The medical examiner had told her Gerry was so intoxicated that she would have been comatose when the fire started. I realized that could not be because she did not drink. Drinking always put her diabetes out of whack and she ended up in the hospital, I remembered she had told me during the long interview.

"But the police said in the insurance trial that she bought a six-pack of beer every night and took it home," Martin reminded Sallianne.

"She could have been buying the beer for the man who was living with her," Sallianne told Martin.

"While that may be true, and I'm sure it is, who made her so drunk she was comatose, how did they force her to drink that much and what did she drink to make her that way," he asked.

"Why did someone want to kill her," was Sallianne's next question. "They had to have had a very strong reason for putting her out of the picture. I wonder what it could have been."

The state police had already questioned several of the people who had seen Gerry on the Saturday afternoon prior to her death. They had each told the police that Gerry had been in a really elated frame of mind.

"She was so happy that day," they reported, but none of them could say with any certainty what she was so happy about.

Sallianne more or less agreed with Chad and did not believe that the man found in the second fire was Charlie either. It just did not make sense that Charlie would have lived there in that shack for ten years without making contact with his former partner and brother, Chad, or his sister who lived next door or with his sons. Charlie was a social person; he loved being around his family and friends. He could not have lived in utter poverty and darkness for ten years. That house was no more than a tar paper shack and he was used to much finer homes than that.

"There had to have been another man in her life," Sallianne explained to Martin.

Then it struck her with the force of a bat striking a ball that the man in the second fire had the initials of E and M.

"When I asked Gerry what GEM, Int. stood for while I was doing that typing for her, she replied that the G stood for Gerry. She never explained what the E and the M stood for, but I'll bet they were the initials of the man who lived there!"

"You can't know that for sure," Martin cautioned her.

"I know that but I'm betting I am on the right track now," Sallianne replied. "Now it is beginning to make some sense.

"The only thing that does not make sense is why did she have to be killed?" Finally, after sorting out her thoughts Sallianne was able to lie down and rest. Upon rising the next morning she was still very upset so her husband decided to take her on a picnic in a park in another county and walk her around in the sunshine. Maybe a little fresh air blowing through her brain would calm her down, and she needed a day away from her office, he thought.

The little outing did help but it did not answer her questions to Sallianne's satisfaction. Only sure knowledge could do that.

Chapter 11

Arriving at work the next morning, Sallianne made a list of things she wanted answered and where she needed to look to find those answers.

First on her list was a visit to the local sheriff's office. She lifted her phone and placed the call and asked to speak to the sheriff himself and not one of the deputies.

She asked him to call the state police investigators and have them meet with the two of them and his chief deputy in one hour. Sallianne explained to the sheriff that she thought she had arrived at some of the answers that had been plaguing all of them.

The sheriff agreed to make the calls and in due time the four lawmen and the lone newspaper reporter entered the interrogation room (really the dining room of the attached sheriff's residence). One of the state troopers was skeptical but the other had worked with Sallianne on numerous occasions and had always found her to be well grounded with good questions and some answers.

The sheriff asked Sallianne what it was she wanted to talk about. She replied by throwing a bombshell amongst the quartet of lawmen. "Have you looked for or found the fourth body yet," she asked.

The sheriff had been leaning back on his straight wooden chair with its two back legs against the wall. He thumped the chair down to the floor and asked her what she meant by that question.

"Well, I believe if you look far enough that you will find a fourth body," Sallianne said.

"And I know you have never said so, but I suspect that Gerry was a murderer."

"That is the only statement that makes any sense to this case at all," the sheriff replied.

"What," the two state policemen shouted in unison. "How on earth did you come up with that idea?"

"Just think about it like this," she explained. "Think of this whole situation as a jig saw puzzle. You can keep putting pieces in place or moving them around if they don't quite fit but eventually if you keep trying every piece will slip into place and you will have the whole picture."

"For several years I was a faithful friend to Gerry. I respected her requests for secrecy about who was living with her. You both said you thought Charlie had been living with her all that time but I am here to tell you that the man who was living with her and the man you want to identify has the initials E. and M."

By now she had their complete attention. "Please explain," the sheriff asked.

"Well, all those times I did that typing for Gerry she signed her correspondence as GEM Int. She told me one time that the G stood for Gerry but she would never say what the E and the M stood for. I believe those initials belong to her boyfriend."

"Who do you think this boyfriend was," one of the troopers asked her. "And how can you confirm this?"

"I'm going to return to my office and read every story ever written about this case. I am going to look for a man in those stories whose initials are E.M. When I find that article, we will know what his name is," she explained.

"If I find the name, will you guys help me look for him?" she asked. "Yes, we will," all of the lawmen agreed.

Chapter 12

Returning to her office, Sallianne began her hunt for clues to the identity of the mystery man found in the second fire.

She began by reading the stories about the trial of Adam and the dead hunter.

Finding nothing in those stories that would seem to help her solve this latest case, she moved on into the stories that had been written about the insurance trial and it was here on the first front page she opened to read that she struck pay dirt.

Near the bottom of the page was a small story about the guy who did not show up to testify at the trial who had been paid by the insurance company to do so. The story was only about six inches long, spread over two columns.

The headline read, "Edward Morris, where are you". Bingo, E. M. That has to be the missing man, she thought to herself as she read the short story over many times. He was but one of many witnesses who received some type of payment from the insurance company to testify in their behalf.

Smiling, Sallianne knew she had just found the first piece to a long puzzle so she took that story to the copier and printed off the story.

Taking that copy to the courthouse she ran that name against the criminal records index and here once again she got lucky. There were numerous entries against Edward Morris, and all had to do in one way or another with automobiles. Bingo, Bingo, the bells started going off inside Sallianne's head once again. More of the puzzle pieces were being located.

Is it just me or is all this coincidence, she thought to herself. Here is a man who was arrested numerous times for auto theft, title fraud and other auto related incidents. Could it possibly be the same man?

She looked in the background checks investigators had made against Morris that were still on file relating to these old charges. Now she knew she was on the right track. The Edward Morris she was looking at was 32 years old when he was last arrested and that was just a little over ten years ago, making him now just over 42 years old.

Going back to the same criminal charge book she looked up the names of all four of the Jones boys to see what would turn up on them.

Surprise, surprise, what she found was that Edward Morris and Fred Jones had served time in the same jail cell at one time a few years back and they had become good friends. One more piece of the puzzle had been found.

Edward Morris had lived only about four or five miles away from the Jones home at the time of most of his arrests and now she learned he had been friends with the oldest Jones boy. What incredible luck. She now had a viable suspect.

She obtained the social security and driver's license number from the case file and headed back to the sheriff's office with that information.

Asking that the jail dispatcher check the national files for this Edward Morris having this social security and driver's license number put the dispatcher in sort of a bind.

"We are not supposed to do anything like that unless one of the deputies asks us," he told Sallianne.

Sallianne explained what she was up to and that the sheriff and state police investigator knew that she was doing some sleuthing about the Jones case. After the dispatcher heard her tell him this, he decided to check the name on the national files but would do it kind of on the QT.

Within seconds after he entered the information, he got a hit and a possible location of the man Sallianne was looking for. It appeared the man now lived in Georgia near a little town called Shiloh. Another piece was located. It was beginning to round out her puzzle rather nicely, she thought.

Tearing off the telex paper she slipped it into her file and told the dispatcher she would be getting back with the sheriff and the state police in a day or so. She returned once again to the newspaper morgue to dig out as much other useful information as she could find to substantiate her case against this Edward Morris.

But after having read every word ever written about all the Jones' affairs in the newspaper, she could discover nothing else useful and closed the book sadly.

"I know there is more there, I just wonder what it is I'm overlooking," she mused.

She sat for some minutes and then decided to read further back in the bound history books to see if there had been anything else that could have sparked the events of the past ten years.

This turned out to be another stroke of genius and added one large piece of the puzzle.

Beginning about six months prior to the earliest fire she began going through the morgue files page by page looking for anything, no matter how large or small it might be, that might have something to do with the current case.

It was boring, dusty work and she was beginning to think she would not find another thing of consequence when there it was, just what she had been looking for but not really expecting she would ever find.

Only one month prior to the first fire ten years past she discovered that the general store belonging to Chad Jones had been broken into during one foggy October night.

According to that very short story, the following is what Chad reported to the police and the newspaper about his burglary.

Chad said that he could not determine if anything at all had been taken. "I only keep about $20 change in the register at night and it was all there. There was no vandalism or anything like that. I like to never found anything missing at all and I'm not sure there is anything missing without doing a complete inventory and my loss is hardly worth going to all that work. Nothing else was disturbed or stolen except some very small items like candy, small hand tools and, I believe but am not sure, a package of poison I keep that the farmers use to eradicate groundhogs that are eating and damaging their crops. My wife could have sold that to someone else so I'm not even sure it was part of the stolen items. There was so little taken that I didn't even notify my insurance company," Chad reported.

"Who had keys to the store," he was asked. "There were only three keys out," Chad explained.

He had one, his wife had one to use only in an emergency and his former partner/brother Charlie still had one, he replied.

"There does not appear to be any forced entry. I believe someone used one of those keys to gain entry," the police would later speculate.

"Do both you and your wife have your keys now," Sheriff Schneider asked Chad.

Chad showed the lawman his own key and picked up the phone and called his wife to make sure she had hers. "Yes, it is right here," his wife said.

"I wonder why they would break into your store and take only these small items, what could they have been looking for?"

It was not something that Chad could answer. He did not know but Sallianne thought she just might know the answer to that question and added that information to her puzzle pieces.

Sallianne made a copy of this story and copied the name of the poison in her notebook then consulted with a local university chemist to see what the composition of it was and how it was used.

She was told that normally the poison was simply mixed with water and when the water was added it became a tasteless but deadly gas. It could be mixed with other solubles with the same, only slower results, she was told.

"Farmers generally pour these granules down in the groundhog holes when they find them in their fields, then pour a few buckets of water down on the granules. This very quickly becomes a deadly gas and the groundhogs are killed right in their holes and do not have to be disposed of," she was told. "They dig their own graves," he laughed.

"Could it be mixed and activated with, say, yellow mustard or mayonnaise or something like that," she asked the scientist.

"Yes, it could have been," he replied. "There would easily be enough water in those mixtures to activate it but it would be much slower. Lots of water added to the granules works much faster.

Therein contained all the information and evidence she needed to go back to the sheriff's office.

Calling Sheriff Schneider to ask him to set up another meeting with the state police investigators she explained that she might have arrived at the answers they all were looking for.

Chapter 13

When Sallianne arrived at the sheriff's office she found that state trooper Darren Andrews was there along with another trooper he had been working with in trying to solve the puzzle. Also present was Sheriff Schneider along with his deputy who had originally questioned Sallianne about what she knew about the case.

Trooper Andrews was a good looking man about the same age as Sallianne, around 30 years of age. He had the most incredibly beautiful blue eyes she had ever seen, was a former Marine, still nicely muscled and well-toned and was so nice to everyone that if he had ever arrested her and questioned her, she was sure she would have spilled her guts just looking at him. She had wasted many an hour after their regular Friday afternoon talks being teased around the office for thinking about him. Nearly every Friday afternoon for the past few years since she had been writing about the activities of the local police departments, he had stopped by to review details with her on several of his on-going cases. He trusted her to save back those stories that were still not being made public and she had never violated that trust. In return, she could discuss and ask him nearly any question she might have about any member of the various police departments she reported about and know that it would go no further than Darren's ears. When those cases he had asked her to hold back on were completed she already would have the background information she needed from him to write a good story. This method worked to both their benefits. He often picked her up from the office and took her to crime scenes with him. In return she would be on hand to take and develop the evidence pictures that he would need.

After each of them at the meeting had gotten either a cup of coffee or a soft drink they sat around the dining room table, prepared to hear what Sallianne had to say.

She began by asking Trooper Andrews what he had discovered. "Not much, actually," he replied.

"I know that oldest Jones boy, and probably the youngest one also, is involved in this somehow. I just feel that in my bones but I cannot prove a thing," Trooper Andrews added.

"Do you think he actually killed his mother," Sallianne asked.

"Yes, I think it is entirely possible that he did just that but he denies having a thing to do with her killing and I am having trouble actually placing him at the scene of the second fire."

The sheriff spoke up and said that was silly, "That boy would not have killed his own mama. They loved each other and she stood by them boys through thick and thin. Just look how often she came to the jail to bring Adam his cigarettes. Why, she was here every single day he served and she like to drove me crazy," he said.

"I have to agree with the sheriff this time," she told trooper Andrews. "I know you and I have discussed this possibility many times and I always agreed with you that the oldest son had perhaps killed his mother, but now I no longer think he did."

But it was a proven fact, Sallianne pointed out to the sheriff, that kids killed their parents every day and parents killed their kids every day. Family members kill other family members for no reason at all.

"Remember that murder in the western part of the county many years ago," she asked the sheriff. "That was the one where the son shot and killed his dad and mom along with wounding the hired hand?"

"The hired hand had been seated at the dinner table with the man's parents when the adult son walked inside to eat his dinner. The son had carried his rifle inside with him and upon seeing his parents sitting at the table, opened fire and killed both of them, but only wounding the hired man in two places before he made it through the back door to safety.

The hired hand called me on the fiftieth anniversary of that shooting and said he wanted me to write his story and I did. This happened after the first house fire at the Jones house.

"The hired hand told me how he had run from the house, in much pain and bleeding from the wounds in his arm. The hired hand was successful in escaping the house after the shooter's gun had jammed, preventing him from finishing the job. He ran through a nearby cemetery and saw that one of the above ground crypt's doors was ajar and he had hidden inside it.

"All during that day he could hear but could not see what was taking place outside, but he could hear what he thought was a shoveling sound.

"Later on that same day he heard a final shot from inside the house and then moments later the house was torched and went up in flames. Since there was no such thing as an organized fire department at that time, by the time the bucket brigade of private citizens and neighbors arrived to put out the fire, the house was a total loss. Many of the bucket brigade lived up to a mile away so it took some time for them to make their way to the fire scene.

"Two men's bodies were found in the ashes, but no female body was found.

Neither the mother's body nor the son were ever seen again.

"The survivor of that massacre said he thinks the son buried his mother's body in the already occupied grave of someone else who had been dead for many years.

He said he and the son had been busy for several weeks clearing brush and canebrakes from the old graveyard. It had been the hired hand's job also to reset the tombstones that had fallen over. The dirt they used came from the new storm cellar that was being excavated next to the house.

Many of the graves had at one time been filled with the remains of the dead that had been placed in wooden caskets. As that wood had rotted and fallen in, the graves had sunk somewhat making them susceptible to rainwater and snow melt damage. The two men had been busy for weeks filling the graves back in and reseeding the tops to prevent any more erosion. They had only worked on that job in their spare time so there were many old graves with disturbed tops in that cemetery.

"It would have been an easy job for the son to place his mother's body in any one of those graves and no one would ever have been any the wiser," Sallianne related to the lawmen. "It is for sure the person already occupying that grave did not object, and that is why her body was not found in the fire. The cemetery was very old, the hired man told me and there were no descendants of the dead buried there still living around there as far as he knew. And the family that died on that day left no living relatives, so there was no one who would object."

"After the fire, the son was never seen again, nor the body of his mother ever found.

"And why would anyone want to look into one of those graves? A grave would have been a perfect place to hide a body. And, you could tell how many of them were in the process of being repaired and disturbed."

"He believes the son set that fire and was killed in the fire either accidentally or deliberately," Sallianne related. "But he had no idea what had enraged the son to the point that he would shoot both his parents, the hired hand and most probably then committed suicide after setting fire to the house."

The sheriff smiled as he recalled the incident as told to them by Sallianne. "This was a perfect example of children killing their parents," he explained. Trooper Andrews reminded the others that Sallianne had also been instrumental in helping him solve another similar mystery not long ago in which the wife of a well-to-do gentleman shot his head off and left his body in their home for two weeks before she, too, had the house burned down in an attempt to obscure that evidence.

"That was the case where you were to take the official pictures for us as we searched the ashes, Officer Andrews reminded Sallianne. "Only you found out you had forgotten to put film into your camera," he laughed.

"The wife had killed her husband and hired her boyfriend to burn the house down. As his reward for committing arson he was given the gun with which she shot him. We never found that gun in the fire. If she had left it there, it might have gone down as a suicide, but since there was no gun and he had been shot, we knew it was murder.

"This was just another incidence of a wife killing her husband," Trooper Andrews explained.

"She only had to spend four years in prison for her part since she convinced the jury it was done in self-defense since he had been abusing her."

"Anything was possible when a great deal of money was involved and two million smackers is a lot of money, as it is in the Jones case," she said.

"Yes, that is true, but I would have a very hard time believing that Fred killed her, or any of the other boys for that matter," Sheriff Schneider said.

"Well, let me run what I have discovered by each of you and see what you think and let us see if any of it will link this whole puzzle together. I think it is a pretty good hypothesis," Sallianne said.

"I want each of you to go along with me and picture this as a jigsaw puzzle as I have been doing. As I lay out the pieces before you, try and place them where they belong in this puzzle," she asked them.

First, she explained how she had gone back and read through every story again that had been written about all the many cases the Jones family had been involved in over the past several years. Many of those stories she had written herself but had forgotten the essence of them. Some were written just before and after the first Jones fire by other writers before she had been hired to work at the newspaper and she could not remember what had been in those stories and decided she needed to refresh her memory about everything.

"I found some really interesting stuff," she said.

"Have any of you ever thought that perhaps Gerry could have killed her husband," she asked.

"No way," the state police said. "That little old lady could not hurt a flea." 'Here is how I have pieced the whole thing together, and I think it is highly likely that she killed Charlie herself or helped someone do it," Sallianne said.

"I think she was influenced and abetted a lot by her boyfriend."

Gerry's having had a boyfriend was a new idea to all the lawmen. They had never considered that as a possibility, but Sallianne was convinced she did indeed have one and that he was much, much younger than Gerry.

It had been common for centuries for older men to have much younger women as lovers and wives, but it was uncommon for women to have what would one day become known as "toy boys."

"Charlie was known as a womanizer by all his friends. I picked up that tale from several places, and it was not just a rumor either. Some of the family friends said that Gerry had come home one day and found Charlie in bed with his girlfriend, Mabel Miller.

"Not only was he in bed with another woman, he had her in his and Gerry's marriage bed. It was that day that their marriage officially ended Gerry had told certain family members who related it to me.

"As long as Charlie was making money and sharing it with her and the boys, she never left him, but she made his life entirely miserable from that day forward until the day he died.

"Charlie had tried to keep Gerry from learning the value of and even the fact that he had a life insurance policy, but she had taken a phone call for him one day from his attorney who left a message for Charlie that said she was paying his life insurance premium for him again and he would need to stop by her office and repay her.

"Gerry gently questioned this older woman attorney about the policy and its value and learned it was written for two million dollars face value and that it had no clause in it against suicide. Even if Charlie killed himself, his beneficiary would receive this money.

"This was the first indication Gerry had that things were not so rosy for her robust husband and it gave her some ideas about how to cash in on it. She began right then making plans to put him out of her life forever.

"One day Charlie had returned from a business trip, and exhausted, had just fallen into bed.

"Gerry, knowing that when her husband was that tired, he would sleep the clock around, removed his key ring from his pants pocket. She quickly and quietly removed the key she knew belonged to the general store he had sold to his brother. Hurrying to a key maker in a nearby small town where no one knew her, she asked that the key be duplicated. Once she had this key in her possession, she quietly replaced the original on Charlie's key ring.

"He had not only been unfaithful to her many times, even bringing his sleazy bitch into her house and into her bed, he had also become very physically abusive toward her. He never left a mark on her body that could be easily spotted by her friends. He always made sure that all the bruising was done where her clothing would cover it and the bruises would barely have time to heal before new ones were placed on her body. This is a time-honored ploy of a wife beater. Gerry was afraid to turn him into the sheriff at that time because the sheriff was Charlie's brother. She knew the brother would not believe that her husband had beaten her on frequent occasions. The men in that family stuck together, so she had bided her time.

"Once she had discovered the material value of his insurance policy, she made up her mind to stop all the abuse and infidelity and get even with Charlie at the same time.

"One misty night about a month prior to the first fire she dressed in dark clothing and secured the store's key inside her purse and drove to Stoneville to pick up her as yet unknown male friend. Acting as his lookout, she made sure he would not be detected as he sidled up to the back door and quickly let himself inside. He already knew where the poison Gerry needed was located because she had entered the store and talked to Chad several times, making it a point to casually walk around and locate it. She had gone over its location time and again with her male friend. He felt he knew the layout of the store as well as she did before he entered the store. This night it required only a couple of minutes to pocket the small package, grab some other small items he could carry away in his hands to make it look like a legitimate burglary and leave the store, locking it back behind himself as he left. He quickly walked around the corner from the store and stepped inside the Lincoln Town Car that was waiting with Gerry at the wheel with the motor running. Holding up the small package he grinned at Gerry and she knew that everything was going as she and her friend had planned it.

Gerry dropped her friend back off at the local tavern and said she would get in touch with him again very soon.

At this point the state trooper asked Sallianne how she knew so much about the case and she explained how much Gerry had inadvertently told her over the years.

"I just kept putting it together like a puzzle as I explained to you earlier, as I read the stories about that family," Sallianne said. "Now I believe I have pretty much the entire story."

Continuing with her detailing, she asked if the police could provide her some personal protection if anything she told them became public knowledge.

"We will do everything in our power to protect you," Trooper Andrews said. "Please continue with your story."

She explained about the missing insurance witness and who she thought that might have been and why.

She reminded her audience about the typing she had done for Gerry and the initials she always used as a signature and how she had explained what those initials meant.

"I'm sure you can contact the U. S. Patent office and ask whether or not they have anything on file with those initials," she explained. "That would verify that I am telling you the truth. Perhaps if she did actually mail the papers to them, they could send you a certified copy."

"We'll do that right away," Trooper Andrews assured her, jotting himself a note to do so in his notebook.

"I believe this is the man who had been living with her the past ten years. He and her oldest son had become good friends while they were serving a stint in the local jail for some minor offense and that friendship had continued once they had been released. This man had even stayed in the Jones family home for some time off and on over the years. Gerry and he had developed quite a close friendship on their own that no one else knew about except her.

"He realized that she had developed quite a crush on him, even though he was the age of her oldest son and he took advantage of that fact.

"Gerry had inadvertently let slip to him the value of the insurance policy on the life of her husband and the two of them had laid their plans to collect that money and share it. It would be at his urging that Gerry started helping him make plans to kill her husband and make it look like suicide and then the two of them would marry as he had promised her they would.

"On the afternoon of the first fire in which the unknown man was found in the ashes, Edward Morris rode with Gerry to the nearby town to pick up the fish sandwiches. On the way home they had placed the deadly poison inside the buns holding the fish, rewrapped them and replaced the sandwiches back in their original sack. The strong fishy smell masked the odor of the poison in the mustard.

"But because there was so little moisture in the mustard, the gas did not expand as it was expected to do, but that was fine too, maybe even better than they had planned it. They

111

decided to leave it as they had prepared it and she drove on into Stoneville and dropped him at the corner tavern explaining that she would drive home, leave the sandwiches, and return to pick him up.

"We will go to Fred's house and visit for a while. He still does not know that we are close friends so he will accept the fact that we are just friends when he sees us together," she explained.

"Edward Morris went along with her plans and decided to have a beer at the local tavern until she returned to pick him up. A Pabst Blue Ribbon would go down really well, he thought a bit nervously.

"Everything went as the two conspirators had planned and he had managed to drink two Pabst's before she returned.

"They drove to Fred's house and it was there that she was located when the fire was reported.

Trooper Andrews asked Sallianne who the man in that fire had been and Sallianne explained that Gerry had told her that when she returned home with the fish sandwiches that she had found that Charlie had brought another of his down-trodden drunken friends home with him and that he was passed out on their couch sleeping off a drunk. She didn't know his name nor care who he might be. He was the expendable part in her plan but his body would come in handy. He was almost exactly the same size as Charlie so perhaps that would be an added advantage.

"She told Charlie about the fish sandwiches being there on the counter for his supper. If you remember, he had asked his cousin, Jim, to come in and share one with him when he had stopped by while he was raking leaves. But Jim had wanted to hurry home and spend his anniversary with his wife. So, since Jim could not stay, Charlie had decided to eat alone.

"Charlie very quickly became incapacitated and was near death in only a few seconds as a result of eating those poisoned fish sandwiches.

"Gerry and her friend Edward Morris had driven back home and backed her Lincoln inside her home's garage and had placed Charlie's by now dead body in the car's trunk. The trunk was very roomy so there was plenty of room for even Charlie's man-sized body to fit inside it. What they thought was the dead body of the drunk man was placed on the floor of the garage, where they piled some flammable items and some accelerant over this material and lit the fire. They had then driven the Lincoln outside the garage and closed the overhead door prior to setting the garage on fire so they could quickly flee the scene. No one to their knowledge had ever known they had been back to the house. There were no close neighbors who would have noticed their actions. "If you can remember back to about 1970, there were only about 7,000 people in the whole of Green County. Their chance of being seen by a passerby was very slim.

"It was only after committing this act together that they went to Fred's house and they had been there only a few minutes when a deputy sped up to the house and told the family about the fire at Charlie's garage.

"Fred did not know the circumstances and he hurriedly rushed his mother to the fire scene where they were told that a body, or what could more closely be defined as what little bit of tissue that was left of a human body, had been found in the blaze and that it was most likely Charlie they had found.

"Gerry put on a great act, falling to the ground and crying loudly for her Charlie," Sallianne explained.

"It would be many hours later that Fred would learn about his mother and her friend plotting the demise of his father. But Fred was not too distressed upon hearing the details because he and his brothers were becoming more and more aware that their father was quickly going broke and he could no longer finance their extravagances and each of them would be losing their luxury automobiles and maybe some of their homes.

"Gerry also told her son how his dad had been beating her up, making sure that the bruises were not visible to anyone other than herself and how she had found his girlfriend in their bed. To back up this story she showed the sons some of her healing bruises.

"Charlie had been having a poker party at the house one night and I heard him offer my body to one of his poker buddies in exchange for a loan so he could keep playing. That man raped me repeatedly and Charlie never raised a hand to stop him," she had explained to her son.

"So Charlie was prostituting her to his friends and beating her up and abusing her in many ways," Trooper Andrews asked?

"I have heard about some of that happening also," the sheriff responded. 'I guess I just didn't want to believe it though."

"Yes, he was doing all that along with going broke. Gerry was scared for her life and for the lifestyle Charlie had let her and the boys become accustomed to enjoy," Sallianne said.

"This story just gets weirder and weirder," Trooper Andrews said. "And that is not the end of it yet," Sallianne said.

"She might have gotten away with voluntary manslaughter if she had stopped at that point and explained to the police why she had killed her husband. She might even have claimed she did it in self-defense. But she didn't stop there. She had already involved her much younger lover and then she asked two of her sons to help her conceal his body so they could collect his insurance money. That is conspiracy to commit murder any way you look at things."

"When, where and how do you believe she concealed his body," Trooper Andrews asked.

"Well, let me ask you something first. Didn't you tell me at one time that in order to help you resolve this case you had asked a psychic to tell you where Charlie might be found?"

"Yes, I did. She told me his body was buried at a place known as "Five Points.""

"Did you guys ever go there and look for him," Sallianne asked?

"No, no one we talked to had any idea where that might have been; it certainly isn't on any county map. So we figured the psychic didn't know what she was talking about and we didn't follow up on it," Andrews said.

"Well, oddly enough, according to local folklore, if you follow the hollow behind Gerry's ramshackle house about a mile or so back to the southeast you will come to a place where there are five paths the old timers used long before the county's road system was developed," Sallianne explained to the skeptics. "Five ridges with easily walkable paths came together in this location.

Originally these paths were game trails, then the Indians had used them, further wearing the trails on the landscape. Then the white men had come and followed along these same trails. Once the county was established, the road builders followed along many of these worn paths.

"This is the place I believe the psychic was probably referring to because that point where all the roads came together was known to all the old-time locals as "Five Points," Sallianne explained.

"Well, I'll be damned," Trooper Andrews said. "Did she tell you anything else," Sallianne asked. "Yes, she did, but it never has made sense to me." "What did she say?" Sallianne asked.

"She said that for us to find what is there, we first had to look for what is not there. It was a real conundrum that we were never able to figure out."

"Does that make any sense to you," he asked Sallianne.

"Not yet, but I do have my own ideas, maybe it will later on," she answered. "There are a lot of old house places back there in the park that you can still find some evidence of. Most of the places were either burned down or pushed down or left to rot when the owners moved off the now publicly owned land way back in the late 1920s when the state bought it to form the state park. "Some of the old timers took as many of the boards which made up their homes as they could haul away as they moved which means that some of the house places were completely obliterated. They then reused the boards to rebuild their new homes in their new locations. They were mainly very poor, hard-working people so everything they had was precious. Many, if not all, of these

117

old house places had large diameter dug wells to furnish their water needs and cellars and other outbuildings.

"I believe that Gerry had her boys and her lover place Charlie's body down in one of those old wells or in one of the old cellars. That is the only explanation I can come up with that makes sense. No one for sure has ever seen Charlie in the past ten years. Some say they saw a man, and one or two even said it was Charlie, but I think like his brother Chad, I don't think this sociable man could have lived in secluded squalor for ten years right across the street from his best friend and brother and never communicated with him. I think the man these people actually saw was the missing insurance witness, Edward Morris. "Everything I have been able to find out about him fits with the profile I had unconsciously been forming of him over the years as I did that clerical work for Gerry.

"Here was a man in his mid-30s in 1970, a man interested in automobiles to the extent that all his prison time had been occasioned by that interest in other people's automobiles. Please remember that one of the EMTs at the scene of the second fire had told me the police had told him the body appeared to be a male about 42-years-old. Lover Boy was a fairly smart man and could have been exploring or experimenting with new car designs to while away his free time. The man at the liquor store carryout told you guys that Gerry bought a six-pack of Pabst Blue Ribbon beer every night on the way home. The clerk even went so far as to say she was an alcoholic. But I have to differ with you there. Gerry was not an alcoholic. I offered to buy her drinks and she refused my offer saying that when she tried to drink it made her go into diabetic trauma. I stopped by her house numerous times when she did not know I was going to stop by to leave her typing and I never once smelled alcohol on her nor did she in any way act drunk.

"I don't drink at all so I would definitely have smelled alcohol had she been drinking," she explained.

"And besides all that, have either of you ever seen an alcoholic turn down a free drink," she asked.

Those lawmen present had to agree with Sallianne on that point.

"She also knew the problems drinking had brought on Charlie that had contributed to his downfall and their marriage problems. I just do not think she was buying this beer for herself. It does not compute or make sense.

"Gerry's boys visited their mom fairly regularly. They were accustomed to seeing Edward Morris there in her home and maybe some or all of them realized the closeness of friendship had by now blossomed into something more despite their vast 20-year age difference. They really did not mind. She deserved whatever love and kindness she could find so they said nothing to anyone about her younger friend."

To explain how Gerry had been coerced to drink so much that would make her BAC .387 Sallianne described it this way.

"I believe her boyfriend had told her that once the insurance lawsuit had been settled and she had gotten her money he would marry her despite their age difference. And, Gerry, like many other older women who have a young lover, believed him, and fell for this bait, hook, line and sinker.

"This is why she was so elated when talking with her friends the last day of her life. She believed she was going to marry this man whom she truly loved but who did not love her although she would not live long enough to learn that. "This was a ruse on his part. He had no intention of marrying her. Now that the verdict was in and he knew she would not be getting the insurance money, he had changed his mind. She was old! She was not going to be both old and rich! He was not going to marry her now that she would be merely old and not rich, but she did not know that.

To get her to imbibe I think he told her to take a few sips of whiskey to celebrate their going to be married. "I'll take care of you if it turns out that it bothers your diabetes but we need to celebrate," I believe he told her. "Once she got enough alcohol into her system, she could no longer deny his urging to drink more as he even held the glass to her lips and told her to drink. And to help her along he drank quite a lot himself along with her to allay her suspicions. "It did not take long for Gerry to become comatose, both as a result of the hard liquor he was convincing her to drink and because her diabetes began acting up. Alcohol really disturbs someone with diabetes.

"Once she was in this condition, he laid his final plans to rid himself of her. That is when he poured massive amounts of the accelerant throughout the house and over her unconscious body and on the bed on which she lay.

"But because he had drunk so much alcohol himself, he too, was very, very intoxicated. He made his final, fatal mistake by not having the matches readily available to start his fire, so he had to hunt through a kitchen drawer for a box of matches. In doing that, he allowed the fumes just enough time to cause a flashover when he lit the match, thereby killing himself accidentally. It was Edward Morris who murdered Gerry, not one of her sons."

"If you would search the area around Five Points closely, I believe you will find that fourth body that I mentioned to you guys a long time ago. It is there. You just need to find it."

Trooper Andrews had an even better idea. He knew from talking with his friends who worked for the Department of Natural Resources that there were old hand-drawn maps available of the park area which showed every old house place if he could find them.

When the state bought the land to make it a publicly owned state park a cartographer had been hired to carefully map every old homestead and structure within the park's boundary.

They had done so to preserve the history of the area and rather than have to move any old grave sites that a descendant might want to visit again someday. There was a law on the books that said you could not isolate or cut off access to a known cemetery.

The map maker had been meticulous and had not only shown the location of every wood or stone structure above ground that was to be removed, he had

also drawn on the map where every underground structure, such as a cellar or an old water well was located. This would provide a guideline of areas later generations should avoid if hiking became a popular sport in the wooded valleys of Green County.

"He actually took measurements from one corner of each structure to the next. Since most of the old house sites had the houses sitting on piles of stone as a foundation, you can measure from one pile to the next and define each of the outbuilding locations. Every old house of that time and place had a barn, pig pen, chicken coop and yard, a woodshed and usually a cellar along with the dug wells. If you could find one or two of the coordinates, you could locate the others from that."

"I will go to the state library where those maps are believed to be stored and search them to see if I can find a well or cellar that was located near this Five Points area," Trooper Andrews said.

"It may take us a day or two to do this but if we can find those maps, we can probably easily find the remains of Charlie's body if it is where Sallianne thinks it was dumped," he finished.

This working group agreed to meet again the next week which should give Trooper Andrews time enough time to review the maps.

Chapter 14

The next Tuesday found the same five people gathered at the Sheriff's department.

Trooper Andrews was the first to speak today. "I think we have found what Sallianne was talking about," he told the others.

"We found the location of several old abandoned dug wells and cellars, which were shown on the map to be up around Five Points. If Sallianne is right, we can start digging anytime we want."

"Do you think we will need a court order to go there and dig," the sheriff asked Trooper Andrews.

"Might not be a bad idea," Trooper Andrews said as he pushed himself to his feet.

"I'll go ask Judge Stearn right now if he will issue one so we can get started digging. Do you still have that backhoe you used to own," he asked the Sheriff?"

"Yes, I still have it down on the farm. It won't take but an hour or so to go pick it up and bring it there. I don't want to have to be on the long end of a shovel handle so while you are talking to the judge I will go and pick it up and meet you there at her old place," he replied.

Sallianne said she would go back to her office and alert her publisher where she would be for the next few hours and pick up her camera and film. She wanted to make sure she could document their efforts so there could be no questions asked later.

Having agreed to meet at the site of the burned home of Gerry in one hour, the team members went their separate ways.

They each arrived at the specified location within minutes of each other. Sallianne got inside the Jeep with the state troopers and the deputy. Sheriff Schneider backed his backhoe off the trailer and left it until they determined whether they needed it or not and followed the other group into the wooded area in his own jeep.

The state trooper had a good memory and copies of the entire map around Five Points to Gerry's home that showed where the old structures could be found. They agreed to start at Five Points and work toward Gerry's house. After searching around the first house site, they located every structure marked on the map. They found it was an easy matter to locate a pile of stones on which the old buildings had sat and plot them against the map. The cartographer had been meticulous and all the building sites had been easily identified. The old well was just where the map showed it had been but after carefully probing down the shallow well, the searchers found nothing and moved on to the second house site shown on the map.

At the second, third and even fourth house site, they had the same results. It was at the last old house place that Trooper Andrews said, "I think we have found what the psychic was talking about," the state trooper said. "We have found what isn't here."

"What is not here," Sallianne asked.

"The old hand-dug well that is shown on the map is not where it is shown to have been located," Andrews replied.

"Now we just have to find what is here to solve her conundrum." "Remember, I told you that long ago the boys had filled the well in with

brush, rocks and dirt. If you know right where it was supposed to be we can just have Sheriff Schneider take a scraping off the top with the backhoe and see if there is anything to show there was once a dug well here."

"Nearly all the old dug wells were walled up with creek stone or bricks, so even if the well is filled in we should be able to at least see the wall structure once we dig down a ways," Sallianne instructed.

So saying, Sheriff Schneider went to get his backhoe. With the business end extended over the area where the well was supposed to be he began digging. He had to make a couple of swipes in different nearby locations before he saw Trooper Andrews hold up his hand to stop the digging.

"I think we just got lucky," Trooper Andrews said. "That looks like it has been an old well to me. You can kind of see the outline of where old stones were stacked to make the well's wall when it was dug.

"Let's start digging right here. We have to dig down at least eight or ten feet. The map shows this well was about 12 or 13 feet deep. After we get eight feet deep we better start digging with our shovels," he told the others.

It took Sheriff Schneider only a few minutes to dig the hole down eight feet.

"Hold it, I think I see something," Trooper Andrews said. "That looks like bone to me," he said.

"Okay, guys, let's start digging with our shovels now."

Sheriff Schneider moved his backhoe out of the way and picked up the extra shovel that the troopers had brought for him to use.

"Hold it again," Andrews said. "I'm sure that is a skull we are seeing right now. Come around here Sallianne and get a shot of this. We'll know more in a few minutes, but I want a picture of this every step of the way and before the ground is disturbed too much."

Sallianne adjusted her light meter to account for the shade in the wooded area and took several pictures of the "bone" now showing through the dirt. Instead of being white, the bone had turned a light tan color from being buried in the clay dirt for ten years.

Once she had documented this evidence, Trooper Andrews and the others carefully excavated the dirt from the bone to discover that it was indeed a human skull.

They continued to excavate and photograph until the entire skeletal remains were now showing. Every bone was exactly as it had been in life since none of the skeletal remains had been exposed to the elements or to scavenging animals.

The skeletal remains had sort of slumped downward over the years as the flesh had rotted away from the bones and the brush and debris had rotted making room for some movements. It now appeared to be almost in a sitting position as one looked at it.

What a lucky stroke this had turned out to be. Surely it would lead to the conclusion of the mystery that had fascinated everyone involved with it for the past ten years.

"There is your fourth body, Sheriff," Sallianne pointed out to him. "Right like I said you should find. If that jaw has a gold crown on a front tooth, that is Charlie. I know in my own bones that it is," she said.

"I think you are probably right, there is the gold cap on the front tooth," Sheriff Schneider said. "We have never used that gold cap as an identifier to the public. I just can't believe that you were able to piece this whole thing together like you have done just by reading news stories in those old papers." "I'm surprised I could do it too, but I had more to lead me than just those dusty old sheets of newsprint. I had my memories of what Gerry had been telling me without my even realizing the importance of what she had been saying," she said, "And, I have spent about 75 percent of my time during the eight years I have worked for that newspaper on this one case. You guys have had to pull off it many times to solve other crimes. I didn't have to do that. I just continued on and on with this one crime.

"It wasn't until after that second fire at Gerry's old house when your deputy asked me to think about what I didn't even know I knew that this stuff started falling into place for me, like that jigsaw puzzle I equated it with earlier.

"Without his asking me that one question I probably never would have thought any more about the case," she said.

"When I recalled how Gerry had signed GEM, Int. on all the correspondence I typed for her it made me remember my feelings toward that mystery man."

"Well, I'm glad my deputy had the good sense to ask that one question then," Sheriff Schneider responded. "By the way, Trooper, did you get a reply back from the patent office?"

"Yes, we got that just a few days after our inquiry. It was just as Sallianne had said we would find it," Trooper Andrews said.

Sheriff Schneider now sent his deputy back through the woods in his jeep to Gerry's place where the deputy's car had been left.

Before the deputy could leave the scene, the sheriff instructed him, "I don't want you to talk to a single soul at the office. You are to go straight into my office when you get there, shut the door and put a call through to that same dumb-ass forensic pathologist who has identified the last two dead men as Charlie. You tell him I said for him to get his sorry backside out here with any team he needs to put together and take a look at this skeleton. We believe it too is Charlie and you can tell him I said that. But remember, do not say one word, and I mean just that, to another person. You come right back here when that chore is done.

"If I go back to that office when we are finished here and find it has been invaded with a horde from the news media because you shot off your big mouth to someone in that office, I will fire you on the spot. This story belongs to

Sallianne. Without her assistance we would not be anyplace near to solving this case."

The deputy walked away knowing it was quite a ways back to the patrol car. He knew he would do just exactly as the sheriff had advised him. He needed this job.

Chapter 15

It took the forensic pathologist and his crew of three the rest of that day and most of the second day working under a tent shelter to completely examine, document and remove the bones.

"Since we have a complete skeleton, I think I can determine very easily whether or not this might be the missing businessman," Dr. Parker said.

"I still have the x-rays on file that I used on the second body. The gold capped tooth is a dead giveaway. From the shape and size of this one, I can almost say with certainty that this is the man we have all been looking for but we will know for certain when I have completed my examination of the bones at my lab."

The Jones boys had not been taking any chances when their mother's body and the body of the man had been found in the second house fire. They had immediately had the remains cremated and their ashes scattered in separate places so no one could ever examine them again.

Despite the deputy not speaking a word to another soul other than the pathologist, by the time the exhumation was completed and the lawmen returned to the sheriff's office, the word had gotten out. Perhaps it had come from Dr. Parker's own office. Sheriff Schneider's law enforcement building was bursting at the seams with media types when he got there. Several of the vans outside his office had large round antenna dishes on them to provide live news feeds back to their television offices in the city.

"No comment," was his only comment to these media types as he made his way into his crammed office and threw out everyone who did not work there. After he got them all outside, he slammed the door closed and demanded that none of them be allowed back inside his quarters.

Since they could not get to the sheriff and the county prosecutor hadn't been invited to the exhumation, the media moved across the street to the newspaper office to hound the reporter there for a while.

Sallianne had been sequestered in her office up an open staircase to the second floor. Her boss and publisher placed himself at the foot of those stairs to protect her from the horde and to give her time to write up her stories. He knew she had the story of this century in this state. Sobering up and acting gruff suited him and he was able to keep the pushy news crews and their cameras off the stairway.

They begged for pictures that might be on file but George refused to give an inch. "Those pictures and those stories belong to this newspaper. I will not share them with you."

It took Sallianne until just after nightfall that evening to write the remaining words to her story. Once they were written and handed over to George an exhausted Sallianne climbed out a back window to avoid the television crews parked out front and slipped down an alley to where her car was parked and drove home.

The next day her work was splashed on television screens across the country and even into London and Paris. She won many press awards for her stories and after the furor of what she had accomplished wore off, she purchased the newspaper from George and he retired. She continued writing for that same little hometown newspaper for many years.

Gerry's boys were let off with little more than a slap on the wrist. The most they could be charged with was accessory to murder after the fact and because they had kept quiet since the murderer was their mother and her friend, they only had to spend six months in jail.

Sheriff Schneider retired after his second term and went back to farming. Trooper Andrews retired from the state police post and ran successfully for Green County Sheriff. He served two terms and he remains friends with Sallianne to this day.

Also by
Helen C. Ayers

BEING HEALTHY
CAN KILL YOU

Reading This
Book Could
Save Your Life

HELEN C. AYERS

BEING|
HEALTHY
CAN KILL YOU

This is a hard-hitting exposé of our health care industry. It explores the problems encountered by the author when her doctor's inappropriate care nearly claimed her life. It is written as a warning to others and to spur the medical industry to higher standards. If you are contemplating becoming a hospital patient in the near future, reading this book may save your life.

The second part of the book should be read by everyone wanting to kick the nicotine habit. When you or a loved one succeed in breaking the nicotine habit after reading this booklet, and you can if my advice is followed, please drop me a letter or postcard and tell me about your experience. I would love to know I have helped you kick this nasty habit.

The third portion of this book explains how the author was able to tame her Type II diabetes by following a high protein, lower carbohydrate diet. It also provides some tasty recipes.

https://www.amazon.com/Being-Healthy-Can-Kill-You/dp/B0CK3SDR59/

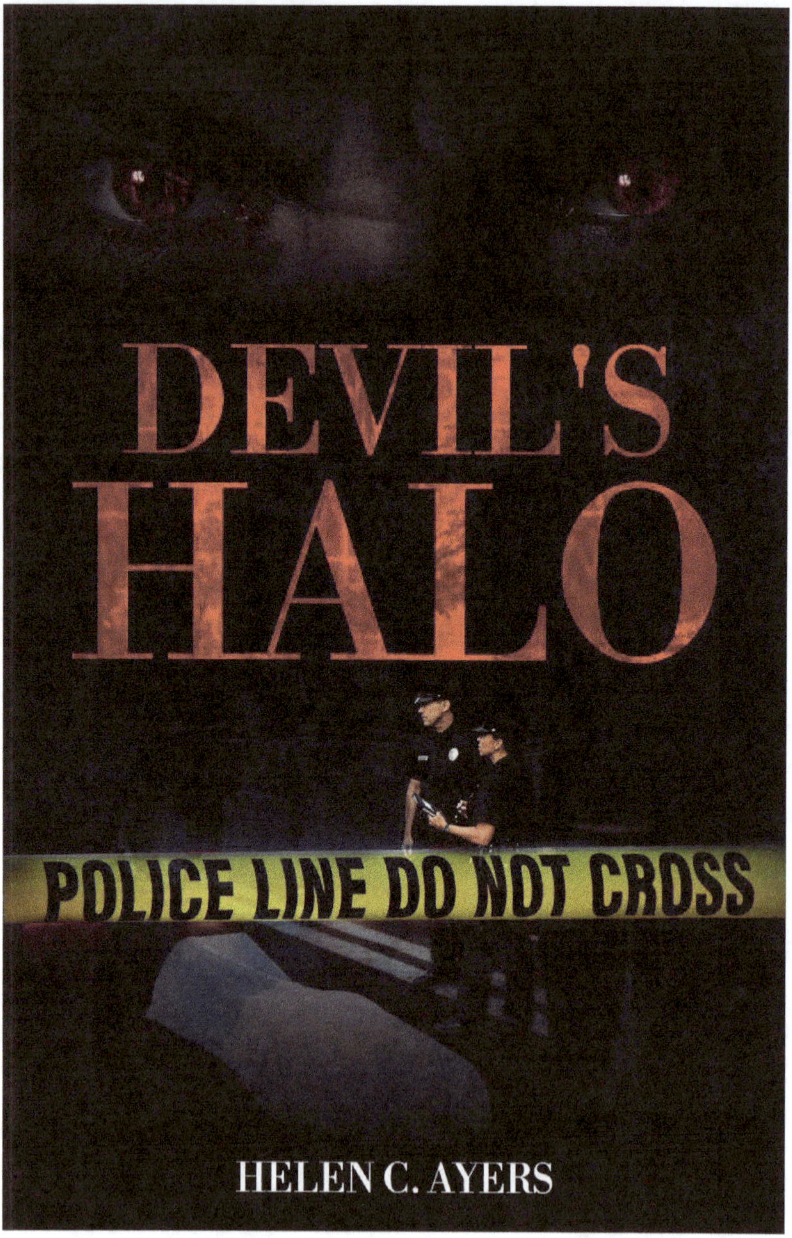
DEVIL'S
HALO
POLICE LINE DO NOT CROSS
HELEN C. AYERS

DEVIL'S
HALO

This book is about the dangers of pedophiles preying on our children whether our homes are in the country, small towns or cities. Bad people are everywhere and are constantly on the alert for an unattended child. We must take more care to teach our children what not to accept from strangers, whether that is candy, ice cream, hunt for lost pets, or any other reason they could be lured into the hands of someone looking to get their kicks by attacking these vulnerable children. Our children must understand they should NEVER talk to or ACCEPT a ride in a stranger's vehicle. By accepting a ride, or believing they will be rewarded for a good work on their part, they can immediately be taken from their hometown in mere minutes and be the object of a gruesome murder as depicted in this book. The writer of this book spent 21 years managing the local newspaper, editing, and lots of writing of crimes and interviewing during those years. She was blessed by having an excellent rapport with the state, local and county police departments as she wrote about crime in her hometown. Many of these kind officers invited her to attend at all kinds of crime scenes, from murder, arson, drug raids, and many other acts of criminal activity. Every Friday afternoon she met with several members of the protectors of our society to have on hand, sometimes as long as six months, the activities they were working on so she would have first bids on the outcome. She met and vetted what they told her by interviewing the county prosecutors and judges. This book attempts to show the horrible outcomes for several children and an adult who did not adhere to the above advice. Just when you think you have solved the puzzles she puts in your way, there is an interesting twist and the true murderer is revealed. Read carefully and see if you can determine who the real killer might be.

https://www.amazon.com/Devils-Halo-Helen-Ayers-ebook/dp/B08X3Q57MF/

How to Order

Appalachian Daughter, $18
The Stuff of Legends, $25
Being Healthy Can Kill You, $20

The books are available online
or any bookseller can order them for you.

You may order direct by sending money order direct to:

Books

7256 Keith Donaldson Road.

Freetown, IN 47235

www.ingramcontent.com/pod-product-compliance
Lightning Source LLC
Chambersburg PA
CBHW071954170626
46813CB00005B/1882